The Immortals' War

Second Edition

The Immortals' War

Kyle C. Bernelle

Illustrations by Robyn Trinkwon

TATE PUBLISHING
AND ENTERPRISES, LLC

The Immortals' War
Copyright © 2013 by Kyle Bernelle. All rights reserved.

This title is also available as a Tate Out Loud product. Visit www.tatepublishing.com for more information.

No part of this publication may be reproduced, stored in a retrieval system or transmitted in any way by any means, electronic, mechanical, photocopy, recording or otherwise without the prior permission of the author except as provided by USA copyright law.

The opinions expressed by the author are not necessarily those of Tate Publishing, LLC.

Published by Tate Publishing & Enterprises, LLC
127 E. Trade Center Terrace | Mustang, Oklahoma 73064 USA
1.888.361.9473 | www.tatepublishing.com

Tate Publishing is committed to excellence in the publishing industry. The company reflects the philosophy established by the founders, based on Psalm 68:11,
"The Lord gave the word and great was the company of those who published it."

Book design copyright © 2013 by Tate Publishing, LLC. All rights reserved.

Published in the United States of America

ISBN: 978-1-63063-761-3
1. Fiction / Fantasy / General
2. Fiction / Fantasy / Epic
13.11.18

Acknowledgements

First, I would like to thank my parents, who taught me how to read in the first place, therefore ensuring that I would get hooked on stories. Second, I'd like to thank an author by the name of Piers Anthony, who communicated with me via email and gave very helpful advice.

DEDICATION

This book is dedicated to Tyler Guevin, Dacoda Anderson, John Wang-Hu, Brian DeCamp, Jacob Andrews (writer of the online comic For Lack of a Better Comic). Thanks for being the funniest people I know.

AUTHOR'S NOTE AND FORWARD

If you do not read this, you will not necessarily be confused reading the story, but you will not have the background knowledge to fully know this book in its entirety. I am writing here to explain as best I can this world of my creation. Let's start with names. First of all, any name I italicize is just the name of a type of a creature, whether it is a humanoid or something else. This just shows that the creature is of my creation, and so you, the reader, knows that the italicized word introduces a new type of being. After that first use of italicization, it will not be italicized anymore, so pay attention to what is and is not italicized. Do not worry though; there will not be too many words of this nature, as I decided that I would pay less attention to creating new races/monsters in favor of writing a thrilling story.

The sun rises in the West, and sets in the East. There is no moon in the night sky. These are two main differences from our world, though those may seem minor compared to any other fantasies present.

The population of this continent is made up of hundreds of races, though there are six main races worth mentioning, for they rule the land. Humans are the first race, and the youngest of all of them. They are the most short-lived, but are very good with creating trading relations between the races. They rule the Southeast, ruling part of the plains, and part of the forests. Elves are the next race, and the oldest one. They are near-immortal, and cannot die of old age, but they can die of natural causes, as well as being killed by normal means. They maintain focus on the biology of all things, especially plant, so they are also associated with herbology. They live in the forests to the South and Southwest. The third race is the dwarves. They are very stocky, and also very short, just as their temper is. They live in the mountains to the West. Dwarves know the most of geology, as they hold all manner of stones in high regard, as well as blacksmithing. Gnomes also live in the mountains to the West, and they live amongst the dwarves. They are also short, though they are much milder than the dwarves. They are the most advanced of all the races, and they share their technology with everyone. The next race is the dimidium (italicized later). The dimidium are beings who walk like any other race, but are dragon-like, for they are covered with different colored scales, have vestigial wings (which are usually removed at birth), and have breath weapons, which are different depending on the color of scales they have, along with other traits of a dragon. They are primarily interested in history, as well as war. They live in the volcanic and ice regions in the North, and part of the desert in the Northeast. The last race is the centaur. They are the tallest of all the races, due to being half-horse, half-human, and live in tribes in the plains to the East, and part of the desert in the Northeast. They have many different fur colors, and are experts with large weapons. They know the geography of Solum better than any other race.

There are many different cities in Solum, though the most prominent are the five ruled by the main races. The human city, which encompasses the castle, is called Moenia. The elven city, which is high in the trees of the forest of Viridis'nemus, is called Nemus Aedes. The dwarven/gnomish city, which is on the face of the second tallest mountain in Solum, Procerus, and holds both kingdoms of the two races, is called Iugosus. The dimidium city, which is partly in the desert, partly in the volcanic region, is called Incendia quod Inculta. The last city, the city of the centaur, is really just the largest collection of tribes in a single area, and is sprawled out across the plains, is called Tribus Terra

It has been many a year where I felt like writing, yet rarely started in the actual act of doing so. I did start once a few years ago, though the copy of it was lost. But still it served a purpose, for it showed me what I want to do with my writing, as well as showed me how much I needed to grow. Now, I feel that I am mature enough to try and write again; this book is the result.

It took me some time to get all of the thoughts from my head in an order that did not appear to be complete chaos, and then even more time to actually write them. The effort and the product, to my eye, are pleasing, and so I release this to the world, for all who want to see. And here we are, you, reading the novel, me patiently waiting to hear of your thoughts on it. My gift to you (though you have to purchase it) is also a gift to myself, in an, albeit, indirect way, but wondrous still. Enjoy.

-Kyle C. Bernelle

Table of Contents

Prologue
 Threatening Storm.. xiii

Chapter 1
 Help!... 1

Chapter 2
 The Unexpected Departure 12

Chapter 3
 Resentful Tide and The Awakening.................... 24

Chapter 4
 Preserved Darkness 38

Chapter 5
 Cold Desolation... 57

Chapter 6
 Meditative Battle... 64

Chapter 7
 Feigned Wroth... 78

Chapter 8
 Isolation... 94

Chapter 9
 Goodly Greed...104

Chapter 10
   Unanswerable Enigma 110

Chapter 11
   War 118

Chapter 12
   Chilling Claws 128

Chapter 13
   The Seeker 137

Chapter 14
   Mesmerization 146

Chapter 15
   Slim Success 155

Chapter 16
   On The Move 166

Chapter 17
   Acrophobia 175

Chapter 18
   Mysteries Solved 187

Chapter 19
   Clashing Forces 198

Chapter 20
   Malevolent Machinations 212

Chapter 21
  The True Monstrosity..225

Chapter 22
  Prelude to a New Beginning 235

Prologue

Threatening Storm

Although all of the enemy troops took the field, no blood had yet been shed. No armor had been dented, and no swords chipped. The enemy infantry had marched to the middle of the battlefield then suddenly stopped. The commanders could not make any sense of it. The troops all had one expression on their face, one of confusion. The enemy knew that its force was twice as large as the one holding the mountain pass, so why not charge and take it?

The soldiers shifted uncomfortably in their wet armor, drenched from the torrential downpour that fell from the sky. They still clutched their bows in anticipation of a charge, though none had yet come.

An archer, Lex, the only female soldier there, saw a

sudden movement among the ranks of the enemy. A line straight through the ranks had been made, enough to fit a large war engine through.

But no war machine came. Instead, a lone figure made its way down the alley made by the enemy troops. In his right hand he held a very long sword. It was straight till the upper part of the blade, where it curved outward slightly, while remaining straight on the opposite side. Both edges were keen. It was thicker than any of the enemies or their own swords, but the oddest part of the blade was that it was tinged green. Its hilt was pure white, and bent in the middle. A large green gemstone rested in the pommel.

The soldiers glanced at each other uneasily. Why would the enemy send out one soldier who was not even of their own? Lex thought.

His armor, totally unlike the uniform plate the enemy had, was a half-plate that only covered the left side of his chest The rest of his body was covered with an unidentifiable black material, with plate armor on the front of his thighs, his right arm, and also his left shoulder. He also wore a hood, hiding any facial feature from view. He was a hired soldier by the look of him, a mercenary.

He did not seem like a normal mercenary, who were characterized by their raucous behavior when coming close to the soldiers they were hired to kill. They would bellow and taunt and generally make themselves a pain in the neck when not close enough to swing their swords. Once they got closer, however, their swords also became a pain in the neck, or rather, a release from all pain as your dead body hit the ground, headless.

The soldiers on the wooden wall blocking the entrance to the mountains grew wary, for as the man grew closer, the air about him seemed to shimmer and distort at his passing, making him appear to be an indistinct blur.

When he was a shout's shot away from the wall, one of the soldiers called out to him. "Do you come with an ultimatum? For if you have, you had better turn around and tell your commanders we decline, for none shall breach this wall!"

His voice was filled with much bravado, but Lex could tell he was afraid by the slight quiver his voice held. When the man kept approaching, one of the commanders issued an open fire on the man. Lex aimed at the man and released her arrow. As soon as the arrows of her comrades took off with a whisper towards the figure, however, the man disappeared, leaving the arrows to hit the ground, making it appear as though a spiny animal had buried itself in there, only revealing its spikes.

What magick…? Lex thought.

The troops on the wall looked at the spot with fear, for they were sure that he was there not even a second ago. Down on the ground below the wall, behind the reinforced doors in the safety of the fort, the soldiers waiting with pikes gasped and shouted for the commanders. Lex glanced behind her and gasped as well. She peered down into the friendly infantry and saw a lone figure standing in the entrance of the fort, standing in front of the door that had not been opened. The officers down below told the soldiers to be calm, but it was hard to do so when they had just seen a man appear out of nowhere, not twenty feet in front of them. Rain continued to pour, and after a particularly bright lightning strike blinded the men for a second, they could see that the man was no longer standing away from them, but he was now a sword's length away! And as he was only a sword's length away, the troops saw that his right hand reached out in front of him, his sword piercing the heavy plate armor of one of the officers in the front of the ranks.

Time stood still, and as the men watched in horror, the officer slumped to the ground, but the man was no longer there. Instead, he was next seen in the middle of the soldiers, standing around the slumped bodies of ten of their number.

Lightning flashed again, and the first three lines of the troops were cut down, lying in the mud, either headless or with deep lacerations in their armor. The troops below started to panic, and ran away, while the archers open fired on the man, who they now saw standing among the swordsmen and spearmen. Many of their shots missed, and instead killed more of their own. The ones that hit the spot where the man stood with his deadly sword seemed to be buffeted away from the figure by a strong wind, though none blew. In fact, all weather had ceased to exist, as now the men realized that the rain had stopped and now only the clouds were hanging in the sky, devoid of all of the fury they had shown not moments ago. The man tilted his head slightly to the right, and half the archers on top of the battlements fell to the ground, dead before they could blink.

Lex looked at her fallen comrades. This mercenary

was more frightening than the tales of a grand dragon surrounding the entirety of Solum that an old elf had told her before as a child. She fearfully motioned for the rest of the archers left on the wall to follow her down to face the man. Instead, some threw themselves off the wall, in hopes of fleeing before the man killed them. What they got were broken bones, and for some, death.

    The rest of the archers on the wall, a grand total of six, counting Lex, decided that they were not enough to harm this mysterious figure, let alone kill him, so they silently agreed to flee into the mountain through a passageway on the wall. Lex and the other archers could no longer see the man but what he did next would have been etched into their minds forever.

    He stood up straight, and glanced at the fleeing soldiers. He felt the forces of magick around him, whirling everywhere in a chaotic pattern. He concentrated on those powers, and bent them to his will. They soon coalesced into a medium sized sphere. Millions of colors swirled around in the sphere. From the chaos came order, though this order was used to create more chaos. As the sphere stopped spinning, the man directed the powers towards the fleeing soldiers. Millions of colored beams lanced out from the sphere to hit each soldier in the back. The soldiers died a wide array of deaths, depending on the color of the beam that hit them. Some lit on fire, others froze in place, some were petrified to stone, while others were shocked as though hit by lightning.

Threatening Storm

The man sheathed his sword in a black sheath across his back. He peered around the fort strewn with bodies, and to anyone watching, seemed to give a deep sigh. He knew of the six that fled so willingly into the mountain, but he did not think it was worth the effort to chase them. He had cleared the fort as asked by the invading army, and so his work was done. He left the fort, silently stepping past the dead. As he reached the gate, he disappeared without a trace

PART I

Chapter 1

Help!

An elf stood over a map that lay on the table in the captain's quarters. The continent of Solum was laid out before him, in all its majesty. Shaped like a giant O, Solum was a continent that had a huge sea directly in the middle of it. No one knew exactly how the sea of Orbis was created, for it had been there ever since the six main races of Solum came on their giant ships across the ocean of Praecingo, which encircled the continent in its entirety.

The six main races had divided the continent into five main regions, one for each race (the gnomes agreed to share the dwarven lands, for they did not require land of their own). The dwarves held the mountainous region in the West, the humans took the plains and

Help!

sparse forests in the Southeast, the elves took the forests to the South and Southwest, and the centaur took the plains in the East. The humans took land in between the centaur and the elves because they had use for forests and vast plains. The last race, the *dimidium*, took the harsh land to the North, which was filled with volcanoes in the Northwest, an icy wasteland in the extreme North, and a huge desert in the Northeast.

Each race held an equal amount of land, as agreed upon by the Council of Six when the first arrived on the continent. The dwarves and gnomes, of course, received twice as much land as any of the other races, due to the two races living within one realm. These races are not required to always stay within their realms however, and were allowed to go where they pleased, but their rulers and kingdoms reside within the realm they rule.

These are not the only races to reside on Solum, however, and there are as many as a thousand different types of beings. The trolls and goblins, for example, are on the ugly side of the spectrum, while mermaids and fairies are more pleasant and less prone to war. There also a number of oddities on the continent, but where they came from is anyone's guess, for some are unlike any other race that anyone had ever seen.

The elf looked up as his cabin door opened with a creak. His first mate, Ferinus, was at the door. "The city of Monstrum is in sight, Captain Nauto," he informed, in his deep, gruff voice. The elf-captain, Nauto, thanked his first mate, and started to head out the door.

The scent of the sea was carried by a slight breeze, and the captain reveled in it. He gazed upon the city and marveled once again at its beauty, for he had been there before.

The city of Monstrum looked magnificent from the deck of the *Ocean's Will*. Nauto beheld the city in its glory. The huge silver and gold gate guarding the entrance of the only port in the city sparkled in the sunlight. The gate was built in an opening in two large cliffs, and marked the entrance into the harbor. Past the open gate he the saw towering buildings made of stone and metal, spearing the sky above them. As they passed the gate, he could see other ships in the port, some big, some small.

None as magnificent as the Ocean's Will, *however*, he thought to himself, as he lovingly stroked the ship's rail.

The ship was unlike any other in the ocean. It had the customary masts at the prow and the stern of the ship, but instead of having a third mast in the center of the deck, there were two masts on both sides of the captain's quarters, sharing one huge sail, with the crow's nest being on top of the mast that was on the stern of the ship. This allowed for the deck to be wide open, and free for anyone's use, so none of the crew had to go around a pillar of wood in the center of the ship's deck.

Being captain of a ship as beautiful as the *Ocean's Will* put pride in a man, or, in this case, an elf, and indeed the ship was beautiful, finely crafted by the elves from the largest of the durus trees in the elven forest of Viridis'nemus. It was given as a gift to him when he rid his brethren of an evil sorcerer that had been plaguing the elves in the forest for over a hundred years. When he received the ship, he set out almost

Help!

immediately to seek a name and glory for himself.

The ship was piloted by many different races picked up from different parts of Solum. The most unique, however, was Nauto's first mate, Ferinus.

This strange monstrosity served as the first mate, and he kept order on the ship. No one had ever seen such a thing before, and Nauto had stumbled upon him after defeating the sorcerer. The beast was in his debt for saving him from the slavery of the wizard. He was at least eight feet tall, had black horns, arms the size of tree trunks, pure white fur all over his body, and pitch black spikes jutting from the top of forearms. Yes, he was a perfect peacekeeper among the crew.

Nauto himself was lean and tall, as were most elves. His face was narrow, but the grin upon his face made him appear both dashing and confident. He possessed a certain stature and stance that made him appear as a noble. He stood straight, and held a presence that commanded attention. Nauto was also graceful; none of his movements wasted as he stood upon the swaying ship.

The ship reached the port, and the men immediately set out tying the ship to the dock. A ramp was set down, and the captain stepped off the ship, inhaling deeply the odors of the dock. Salty, sweaty, and greasy, the exact aroma a port should smell like.

He turned around swiftly and spoke to his crew. "All right," he started. "We will be staying here for a two days. You have already received your pay, as you all already know, and so spend it wisely. Go on and go, have fun, I have business to attend to."

With a roar, the crew rushed passed the captain. By

the time the two days were done, half of them would show back with no money, and the other half would show up drunk, as was a sailor's wont. Ferinus stayed with the ship, for someone had to mind it, and no one would dare tread upon it with that brute standing upon the deck. Nauto nodded to Ferinus, and set off to deal with the merchants in the famous bazaar of Monstrum.

Nauto reached the bazaar in a matter of minutes, as it was close to the docks. Many different smells assaulted his nose, from the spices on the far side of Solum, to the musty wares of an antique seller. Relics of all ages came through this city, as it was the trading post of the world. Large nobles purchased many a trinket, and the poor could find food and shelter. A city for everyone's needs and wants. Nauto walked around, searching for the merchant he wanted.

Anyone who saw the elf could immediately sense that he had a purpose. His long strides, his head held high, his hands clasped behind his back, his fair skin that was a defining trait amongst his people. His long blond hair, split at the sides by his equally long, pointed ears. He was thin, though his clothes did do a good job of hiding the very well-defined muscles that he had earned on his ship, both by helping the crew and by practicing his swordsmanship. A long rapier was strapped to his side, hitting his leg with each step, as well as several daggers, which were well hidden beneath his clothing.

Nauto sensed someone's eyes upon him, just for a moment, and slightly turned in that direction. Nothing but shadows could be seen.

Help!

A thief sized up the people in the crowd. Every one of them rich, but which one would not have enough power to call the city guard to action?

He scrutinized at a very large man, his vestments glittering with gold and jewels. He turned towards a frail woman, her purse making a pleasant *chink* sound as her money bounced around. He saw a tall elf, who glanced at his direction, rapier at side, walking purposefully to an unknown destination.

At last, he turned to another woman. Her hair was black, and just above shoulder length. She held a long staff, and was very pretty. That pretty face appeared confused, as if she did not know what she was looking for.

The thief chose her as his target, for she was new to the city and no guard would be willing to help her, at least not after she had no money to muster support. He started walking towards her, blending in perfectly with the crowd.

At last, after an hour of searching, Nauto found the colorful merchant he was searching for. He waited patiently for some time while he waited for the merchant to be done bartering with a buyer who insisted on getting a lower price. When the buyer finally gave up and walked away, the merchant's eyes alighted upon Nauto. They widened in surprise and the merchant gave out a small, choking sound. Nauto had been cheated by this merchant two years earlier in this same market and he knew that he only returned once a year.

Nauto had bought a jar that the merchant had said would grant any wish after keeping it in one's possession for over a year. So, since Nauto was still green behind the ears about such cheats and liars, he bought it for the pricey sum of one hundred gold pieces. He waited excitedly for a year, and when it finally went by, he made his wish. But absolutely nothing happened. Now he was back to recollect his lost money.

The merchant finally gathered himself and spoke. "Do you have business with me? If not, I was just about to leave…" And with that, the merchant made a big show of cleaning up his stand and packing his things.

Nauto watched in grim amusement as the pudgy merchant scurried about. Finally, after a minute or so, he was fed up with the act. He grabbed the hilt of one of his daggers, and stabbed it into the wooden stand.

The merchant turned around slowly. "I would like my money back for the fraud 'wish jar' you sold me, and I am willing to forgive and forget if I get my money right now," Nauto threatened. "But if it proves that you cannot pay me the money you owe for your lies, the sum of one hundred gold, then there will be a problem between you and me, which can be solved very quickly with this blade."

The merchant gulped audibly, "I have your money right here, I believe." Visibly shaking, he turned around and grabbed a box that contained his earning for that day. He counted out one hundred gold pieces, and slid them over to Nauto.

Nauto produced a pouch and put the money inside.

Help!

"Thank you for paying back the money. I hope we can avoid business transactions in the future." With that said, Nauto walked off, leaving the merchant to stand there quivering.

Nauto made his way through the bazaar, pushing his way through the throng of people. Suddenly, however, he heard a cry for help. He pushed his way through the crowd towards the human woman who bellowed.

The woman had short and curly black hair, a roundish and very attractive face, and carried a staff in her hand. She was shorter than Nauto, as were most humans, and was very petite. He sensed a certain aura about her, however, that made her appear to be larger, perhaps more menacing in some manner.

"What is wrong?" he asked.

"Some thief stole my money!" the woman cried.

He took the pouch from his bag and handed it to the woman. "This contains one hundred gold pieces, but I would suggest keeping it closer to your person." She looked at him in complete shock, and when he asked which way the thief went, she merely pointed without making a sound.

He turned and started off in the direction she pointed in, and behind him he could hear a faint, "Thank you." He smiled and kept walking.

He had no need for money, for on his ship his fortune was already made. Thousands upon thousands of gold coins were stashed away in his cabin, made from exploring underground tunnels and ridding towns of unwanted creatures, such as goblins and trolls. He had come back to retrieve the money cheated out of him only to teach the merchant a lesson. Now he was going to teach the thief a lesson, but Nauto was a kind-hearted elf, and so he would let the thief keep the money he stole, for thieves rarely steal for pleasure, just for need. Although, Nauto would make sure that he never stole again.

Once he reached the edge of the crowd, he saw a figure running in the distance. Being an elf, Nauto was very fleet on his feet and had a grace that allowed him to never stumble. He set off running to catch up with the thief.

When Nauto was nearly ten paces away from catching him, the thief turned into an alleyway. Nauto followed him, but stopped dead in his track when he found that the thief was nowhere to be found. The alleyway stretched for some time, with no other turns, so the thief could not have gotten far, certainly not far enough to reach the end of the alley. Nauto walked cautiously, listening intently for any sound. There was nothing. Nauto looked around in confusion, baffled by the sudden disappearance of the thief.

A figure appeared at the end of the alley, and started walking swiftly towards Nauto. It was the woman he had given his money to.

He called out, "I nearly had the thief, but he turned into this passage and disappeared!"

She ignored him, and walked right past. He turned around, and saw the she had stopped walking five paces away. She was peering intently into a shadowy part of the alley, though to Nauto it appeared that she was looking at a wall, and nothing else.

She reached out into the shadow, and when her hand returned, she held a man by the collar. It was the thief!

Help!

He had hidden himself within a shadow! Nauto knew now that this was no ordinary thief, and also that his was no ordinary woman, for she started chanting and pointing at the man she held.

Nauto realized that this woman was a witch, for she used words of no language he had ever heard of before, and it seemed that she was cursing the thief! Nauto grabbed the woman by the arm to stop her, and she let the man go. She turned towards him, her pretty face filled with a ferocity Nauto did not know she could possess.

"Stop! This man deserves to die! You will be spared, however, since you showed me great kindness before. Though know this, no other creature knows I am a witch, so you had better keep my secret."

Nauto glanced at the man, who was strangely calm against the fury of this spell-weaver. Nauto spoke. "No, this man does not deserve to die for petty thievery, for he probably needs the money he stole. You have already received over twice as much as you lost, so why not just leave him alone?"

The witch looked in amazement at Nauto. "You would have this man live so he could commit other crimes?"

Nauto regared the man with a stern gaze. "Would you promise to never to commit another crime again?"

The man held his gaze for a moment, matching its intensity, and then simply stated, "No."

Nauto eyes opened wide in utter amazement at the man. Here he was, trying to save his life, and he says he will keep committing crimes!? Nauto scrutinized the man further.

His face was nondescript; the only defining feature was his piercing, intelligent, icy blue eyes.

All-in-all, this man was not someone who you would study in great detail; he was someone who your eyes would just pass over in a crowd. Even his clothes were drab; a light brown cloak, with a black shirt and pants underneath. His stature made him seem like a hunter, a he held a certain rogueish quality in his grin.

The witch spoke. "You see? He must be punished to prevent more crimes from occurring, and I must have my revenge."

This time Nauto backed away from the witch, allowing her to do what she wanted, for he was still very befuddled over the man's answer to his question.

The witch started chanting again, and the air seemed alive with energy. The hair on the back of Nauto's neck stood up as the dark magick started to take hold on the man.

Suddenly, another hand snatched out and grabbed the mage, but it was neither Nauto's nor the thief's hand.

An armored figure stood there, glowering at the three of them.

"Stop! As a guard of Monstrum I now place all of you under arrest!" the woman guard uttered.

The witch struggled in her grip, but she could not break free. Three other guards accompanied the woman holding onto the witch. One grabbed hold of Nauto, another the thief, and the last helped the guard with the witch.

Chapter 2

The Unexpected Departure

An hour afterwards found them in a jail cell, with the guard who originally caught them casting a vigilant eye over them. The witch sat in a corner, glowering at the thief and then the guard, switching on and off. The thief was sitting in the other corner, seemingly asleep. Nauto was gazing out the cell's bars, with a desperate look on his face.

"Look, I have done nothing. At my ship I have plenty of gold to pay for my-" Nauto began.

"Quiet!" The guardswoman shouted. "You will not be able to pay for any release until you are put on trial before the magistrate of this city."

Nauto sighed and sat down, his back now to the bars. He glanced at the witch, who was still glaring at the thief and the guard. They had stripped them of everything they carried, which included the materials she need for her spells to work.

Nauto turned his gaze to the thief, who was now awake and staring intently back at Nauto.

"What is your name?" the thief asked. For a human, he had a very slight build, and medium-length black hair, along with a short cropped beard. Nauto supposed he was handsome, but not enough to attract the gaze for very long. Perfect for any would-be thief.

Though this was no ordinary pickpocket. He seemed very experienced, as seen when he blended so perfectly with the shadows in the alley that Nauto had not given them a second glance.

"My name is Nauto," he replied. "What might yours be?"

"My name is Silen." the thief stated. He glanced at the witch, who seemed very intent on burning a hole through him with just her eyes. "What is your name, my dear?"

The witch increased the intensity of her gaze. "Do not dare call me that, cretin!"

Nauto sighed again. "If we are to be in here for any amount of time, I suggest we make nice for now. Would you please tell us your name?"

The witch eyes rested upon Nauto, and they softened some, though they still held some hardness. "My name is Lamia. I come from a long line of magick users, and I came to this city only to resupply my stock of herbs. As you may know, witches use only herbs and words to cast magick spells, unlike other magick-users who use some of their own spiritual energy, which is the power of souls, to produce magick. I was going to go on the next ship out to the Senium Forest, for there is supposedly something very valuable there. Tell me about yourself."

It was more of a command than an inquiry, but Nauto replied with no malice. "I am an elf from the forest of Viridis'nemus. I slew a wizard there, freeing my kin from his evil magick. They gave me a finely crafted ship, for they knew of my love of travel, and so I made my fortune delving deep into caves and underwater grottos and gaining the treasures within. That is why I did not care about the hundred gold pieces I gave to you, for you needed it more than me. If you are in need of a ship, I will gladly offer my services, for I go wherever the wind takes me, and so I do not care where we journey to."

Lamia spoke again. "It seems I must thank you again, Nauto, I will gladly take you up on your offer, and I am very grateful for you showing such kindness, the likes of which I have never known. The use of magick is widely feared, mainly by nobles who do not want their power usurped. Many laws exist decreasing or even forbidding the use of magick, and so my powers must be kept secret. But enough. Thief, what is your story? I would like to know before I exact my revenge on you, which will come soon enough."

Silen laughed dryly. "You will not be doing anything to me for some time, witch, so I suggest you put the thought out of your head." He grew more serious however, and lowered his voice so the guard could not hear. "I am a thief, as you already know, but no ordinary thief. I have the innate ability to blend with shadows perfectly, and take items from a person without them knowing. The only way that you knew, Lamia, was because of your magick. You sensed something was wrong and saw me running, and then proceeded to check your money, which was no longer there. Am I right?" Lamia nodded her head, and the intense gaze of hate reappeared on her face, again directed at Silen.

He seemed not to notice, and continued on with his story. "I am growing tired of this city, for I have been here too long, so if you would be willing to carry a second passenger…" He glanced towards Nauto, who nodded. Lamia's face filled with disgust at the thought of traveling with such a man.

Silen spoke again, "Thank you, truly. I will travel wherever you will, and it seems like you might need a thief on this quest of yours, Lamia, for you do not know what traps you will encounter, of which I am a master of disarming. Though none know me for who I am, I am the best thief in this city, as well as several other places, namely all the ones I have been to. Like I said, no one knows me, least of all other thieves…" he glanced at Lamia, who shot him a dubious look. "…Though I will demonstrate my abilities again soon enough, if you were not impressed before."

The woman guard stood up, and walked out, calling for a recruit to take her place. The recruit, a slightly older woman with long red hair and a very hardened expression, took her place. She was not unattractive, but had a defined jaw. She seemed disciplined. As she

The Unexpected Departure

glanced into the cell however, she only saw Lamia and Nauto, but no third person. She gasped and quickly inspected the room, fearing an escape. Nauto and Lamia knew his whereabouts however, for he was still in the same corner as he had always been, just deeply hidden within the shadows.

The recruit was panicking now, and decided she had better open the cell to do a more thorough search. She fumbled with the keys at her side, and opened the cell. The guard ordered Nauto and Lamia to stay away from the door, as she made her way to the corner where Silen sat.

Her only weapon was a bow on her back along with a quiver of arrows, so she no chance when Silen leaped from the darkness and held a dagger to her throat. Where he had hidden the dagger was the least of the recruit's problems, however, as she stood there, stiff as a post, and just as petrified.

"You will lead us out of this jail, picking up our belongings along the way, and we will hold you hostage until we reach this fellow's," he pointed to Nauto. "grand ship. After that, you will be set free. Understood?"

The guard slowly nodded her head. Her shoulders slumped in defeat. With a dagger behind her, she had no choice but to lead them out of the cell and to their belonging, which were a room over. They grabbed their belongings, and received a stroke of luck as no guards were alerted as they made their way to the entrance of the jail. They went outside, deeply breathing in the fresh air. It was now night and the streets were not crowded. Nauto took the lead, going towards the docks.

They reached the docks with no incident, to their great surprise.

The docks had a strange feel around them, however, for there was no activity, even though there should have been some at night, and the only two figures there were two men standing guard over some cargo. Mercenaries by the look of them, and they looked fierce.

One was a dimidium, one of the race of "dragon men" that was a part of the land of Solum. He had dark green scales that glittered in the starlight and a huge two-handed sword over his back, which he could easily wield due to the extraordinary strength his kind possessed. Unlike most dimidium, who had their vestigial wings removed at birth, this one still possessed them. They were fairly large, and almost looked as though they could support flight, but the way he kept them folded made it appear as though he had no control over them.

The other figure was more mysterious, however. He had one sword sheath on his back, the hilt pure white, contrasting sharply with the black sheath. It was slightly shorter than the two-handed sword that the dimidium carried, though it was somewhat thicker. He wore a hood which obscured his face, and had plate armor only covering the side of his chest where his heart was, as well as on the front of his thighs, his right arm, and also his left shoulder. The rest of his body was covered in some black material; what kind of material it actually was Nauto could not tell.

The Unexpected Departure

The two standing guard over the cargo barely glanced at the small group as they passed, and did not speak. The cargo they were guarding was situated right next to the *Ocean's Will*, and so the group did not have to travel far to reach his ship.

Nauto climbed up the gangplank and immediately saw the merchant who had cheated him out of his money standing on the deck along with two vicious looking characters beside him. They were both huge and burly humans, both armed to the teeth with daggers and swords.

The merchant spoke. "I would like my hundred pieces of gold back, if you would please, and then we will leave peacefully."

Nauto looked at the merchant with incredulity. "You cheated me out of that money, and you expect me to repay you for what is rightfully mine?" Nauto questioned.

"Wrong," remarked the merchant with a smile. "You bought something that was mine, and whether it worked for you or not is of no consequence to me. I demand payment, or things will get ugly between us."

Behind Nauto and the others, the two mercenaries who were supposedly guarding cargo crept up behind them, ready to pounce at any time. Lamia noticed as much, and whispered to Silen, who in turn whispered to Nauto, telling him of the danger from behind. Nauto turned around to see the two men ready to kill them at any moment.

Suddenly however, as Nauto looked upon the two men, an idea sprung into his head. "How much has this slime paid you to do away with us?"

The dimidium answered the question in a surprisingly human voice. "He has paid us ten gold pieces each." Nauto started at the sound of his voice, for the dimidium were notorious with slurring the letter S in their speech.

Nauto looked at them and exclaimed, "I will pay you triple that if you help rid me of this goon who calls himself an honest merchant!"

The dimidium glanced at his companion, and then slowly nodded. They walked past the group and confronted the merchant, along with his two bodyguards. "To you two standing next to that man, I offer the same deal. Will you leave his employment for thirty gold pieces each?"

The merchant laughed loudly. "These two are my fine sons! They will not leave my side for money! They will make short work of these two hired hands, for they are expert swordsmen! Go and kill them all, boys!"

With that said, the two brutish sons ran towards the mercenaries, though the one on the left ran with a pronounced limp. The one on the right met the dimidium two-hander with two swords of his own, but it was soon seen that he was outmatched against the dragon man's strength in arms, and he hurriedly leaped overboard in fear of being killed.

What was more interesting however, was the fate of the brother with the limp. He rushed at the hooded man, who had not unsheathed his sword. Yet when he reached the man he stopped suddenly and looked deep into the man's hood. He stood there for a moment, his face changing into one of glee to pure terror. Then, dropping his swords, he turned around and ran

The Unexpected Departure

screaming off the ship, his limp forgotten.

The merchant looked in astonishment, as did everyone else, at the hooded man. The only one who did not was the captive guard and the dimidium mercenary. The guard looked at the hooded mercenary with recognition, then fury.

The dimidium mercenary walked to the merchant, picked him up, and carried him to the edge of the ship. As the merchant protested and wriggled, the dimidium threw him overboard. A splash was heard below, and the group started to move again. Nauto, keeping his eyes on the hooded mercenary, and went into his cabin. The female guard moved towards the mysterious man, grabbing one of the swords that the cowardly son dropped from the ground. Silen and Lamia still stood staring at the man.

The hooded mercenary turned around, and faced her. The dimidium also turned around, and seeing the guard approaching the man, he exclaimed, "That will do you no good! If you wish to live, stay away from him. If you have some sort of grudge against him, you will never fulfill it, for you will be dead."

The guard, hearing his words, stopped her advance. "This man killed all of my comrades-in-arms when I was a soldier!"

Nauto had come out of his cabin, holding two bags that clinked, suggesting that the contents of the bags were coins. He looked surprised when he saw the look of pure rage on the guard's face, then looked at the hooded mercenary who stood still. "What is wrong? Did this man wrong you in some way?"

She started to advance towards the hooded man

again, paying no heed to Nauto. Her sword was held high, ready to cleave the man in two. Before anyone could stop her, she swung downward, the sword cleaving the air as it streaked towards the man's head.

The dimidium dove towards the ground, and the others, seeing this, did the same. Nauto dropped the bags of gold, and they rolled into the ocean as the weight of the group hitting the deck made the ship tilt.

The sword hit the hooded man's head, and upon impact, exploded violently into millions of pieces. She screamed as some of the sharp sword pieces pierced her skin, and she fell to the ground. The hooded mercenary still stood there, looking down on the guard. He shook his head and waved his hand over her body. The pieces of the sword lifted from her skin, and the bleeding cuts they had made were sewn up by an invisible needle.

The others got up from their positions on the ground, and looked at the mercenary. "What are you?" Nauto asked in a hushed voice.

"He does not speak. We have been together for almost fifteen years and I have not heard him utter a single word in all that time. I do not even know his name, but I call him Atrox. I am called Vis," the dimidium added as he came up behind Nauto.

Nauto introduced himself, and so did the others once they stopped gaping at the mercenary. The guard was still on the ground, unconscious, but the Nauto made introductions for her. Once everyone's acquaintance had been made, Nauto handed the money to the mercenaries.

"A question." Nauto started to say to Vis. "Why were the docks so empty? And where is my crew

The Unexpected Departure

member who was guarding this ship?"

The dimidium replied. "Can you not guess?" Gesturing to the hooded mercenary, Atrox, he explained, "He did it, of course. The docks only held a couple of people and he made them leave by magick. They were there and then, poof, they were gone. The monstrosity who was guarding this ship is down in the hold, unconscious."

A commotion below them prevented Nauto from replying. On the docks, guards were swarming down the docks that lead to the *Ocean's Will*.

"We should get out of here. Do any of you mind if we leave now?" Nauto asked everyone. No one argued, and so he nodded his head and headed towards the wheel. "My crew will have to stay in this port-city awhile longer," Nauto sighed. "They were all good men and I would hate to lose them, but necessity calls for us to do so."

Nauto's face grew stern, and he grasped the wheel, ready to set off. He started to give orders to the group aboard his ship.

"Vis, cut the ropes holding us to the docks. Lamia and Silen, both of you raise the main sail." He looked at the Atrox, who seemed to be looking at Nauto with expectation. "Can you make sure no one gets on this ship?"

Atrox looked at the approaching guards. He waved his hand, and all of them stopped in their tracks, frozen by ice that suddenly encased them. He looked back to Nauto, who paused to stare in amazement at Atrox once again, then set out to steer the ship out of the harbor, for the sails had been raised and any tethers keeping them to the dock were cut.

Nauto expertly steered the ship outside the port, going once again through the glorious gates. Once they were out in the open sea, Nauto gazed behind him, marveling for the last time upon the glorious city. The stars over the grand parapets of the buildings glinted with joy. Nauto was then hit with a curious thought.

*The sky seems to be...*missing *something*, Nauto thought. The absurdity of the idea caught Nauto off guard, and he quickly dismissed it. The night sky is as it has always been, a grand expanse with nothing but the stars glowing in the distant darkness.

Chapter 3

Resentful Tide and The Awakening

The female guard awoke to the swaying of the ocean. She opened her eyes slowly, confused as to where she was. She sat up in the bed she lay upon and groaned. Her head pounded for several moments, but soon went away. She groggily peered around the spacious room. Suddenly, she remembered what had happened. With a jolt, she quickly got out of the bed. She silently crept to the door, of the room, and opened it slowly.

    She peered out into the hallway, which was very long, and saw nothing but more doors lining the walls. She counted ten total doors on each side of the hall. She then looked down and realized she was not wearing her armor. In its place was a nightgown. She glanced back into the room, and saw her equipment in the corner next to the bed.

After putting on her armor, she seatched for a sword or her bow, but neither was to be found. Again, her memories delivered more bad news. The man who had decimated her comrades in the mountain pass was on the ship, and he had broken the sword she had tried to use. The guard sat on the bed in despair, her head in her hands. She knew not what to do, it seemed hopeless to escape.

She then heard footsteps coming down the hall. She sat up, and quickly thought of what to do. Before they reached the room, she made her way to the door and closed it, then waited on the side of the door, ready to ambush whoever came in.

The sound of footsteps stopped right outside her door. With great trepidation, she waited for her captors to open the door, ready to attack. Instead of barging in, however, they simply knocked.

"May I come in?" a muffled voice asked from the other side of the door.

The guard gulped, and stammered, "Y-yes, come in."

The door opened slowly, and as she saw her captor, she threw a punch at the person. It did not connect, however, as the man ducked it in time. He did not respond with a counter hit, however, and instead walked out of her reach.

"Please," the man spoke reassuringly, "I do not mean to harm you." As she looked at him, she realized he was not a man, but an elf, the same one who was in the jail cell at Monstrum. He held up his hands in a soothing gesture, but her rage could not be quelled.

"Let me go!" the guard screamed in anger.

"That would be impossible at the moment."

"And why is that?" she retorted.

He smiled sadly and pointed up. "See for yourself."

With a huff, she stormed out of the room, and made her way upstairs, the elf close behind. As she reached the deck of the ship, her heart sank. The ship was completely surrounded by water, no land in sight. She walked to the center of the deck and sat down, dazed.

The elf sat across from her, legs crossed. "We did not mean for this to happen."

The guard glanced at him, not understanding his words. She looked around the ship, and saw the dimidium and the male thief from the day before. The witch sat down next to them, eyeing her with concern. The guard cradled her head in her arms, cursing her misfortune.

The guard suddenly sat up, and scanned the ship's deck. She looked at the wheel, and there she saw the cloaked mercenary. She stood up and grasped for her bow, which was not on her back. She cursed, and made to run to the man. The elf and the witch stopped her, asking what was wrong. The dimidium and the thief stopped what they were doing to stare at her.

She turned her head to focus on the elf. She seethed with rage. "I was a soldier for the army of Moenia, the greatest of human cities, where my king rules. During the civil war thirty years ago, when the rebel army who wanted to take over Solum for the humans attacked, I helped hold the mountain pass of the mountain Montis, the only mountain in the human realm. We held the pass for a fortnight, but then the rebel army came at us with their full force. We expected it would happen soon, but we did not realize that the entire army had come not to take the mountain pass, but to pass through unscathed."

The elf gaped at her with bewilderment; he was not familiar with human lore and history. Lex explained further, but still held a wrathful stare at the hooded figure.

"They achieved this feat by using *this*," she pointed at him, "this *monster*, who I doubt is even human. The things I have seen him do are horrific, even more so when they were done against my fellow soldiers! He killed almost every single one of us in that pass, and only six people fled his onslaught, including me. We ran into the mountain pass, and we barely won the war after that slaughter. I vowed to kill this man if he ever appeared before me again, and now that he has, he will pay dearly for killing my comrades."

She shrugged her shoulders to free herself from their grip, and she continued to go to the hooded man. The dimidium stood in her way at the bottom of the stairs. "That is ill advised, human. Do you not remember yesterday?"

The guard tried to push her way past him, but to no avail. He was several feet taller than she, and his strength was unmatchable. He held her by the shoulders and watched as she uselessly struggled. The cloaked man still stood at the helm, seemingly unaware of the events transpiring below.

"Vis is right. Please, would you calm down?" The

female witch walked over to the guard, her voice soothing. "My name is Lamia, what is yours?"

The guard glared at the hooded man, but stopped struggling. The dimidium, who she now knew as Vis, let her go. She glanced at Lamia. Lex knew full well that she could not do any harm to the man, and her rage had blinded her. If she persisted, she may end up dying. "My name is Lex." she mumbled in defeat.

Lex looked at the hooded man once more. He still stood at the helm, unfazed by it all. She knew it was hopeless to fight against him, yet she could not help but be overcome by her anger when she thought of the horrible things he had done.

"My name is Nauto." the elf added as he walked over to her. "I am the captain of this ship. The man at the helm is Atrox. Vis and Lamia have introduced themselves, and he," Nauto pointed towards the thief who had broken out of the jail the day before. "is named Silen. We have one more member on this ship, but he is sleeping below. His name is Ferinus."

As if the mere mention of his name had conjured him, a large, hulking being appeared at the top of the stairs. The ship lurched to the side slightly as he made his way over to Nauto. Lex stared at him in fear, as she had never seen such a beast before. He had the appearance of a minotaur, but was much more fearsome.

Nauto saw the expression on her face, and with a slight grin, allayed her fears. "Do not be alarmed; he is not as beastly as he appears."

The beast, Ferinus, uttered a short laugh, and his voice proving to be as deep as the black of his horns.

Ferinus walked up to the helm and relieved Atrox of his duty. Atrox started to then help Vis with the management of the sails.

"Where are we going?" Lex questioned, finally accepting her fate. She could do nothing to change what was to come, although the members of the ship did not seem as if they had any evil intentions, so she felt mildly safe.

"Follow me down, and we will discuss it while we eat." Nauto stated. Lamia and Lex obliged, and followed him down the stairs.

Vis, Silen, Atrox, and Ferinus were still up above, helping the ship along. Atrox knew what he was doing, though it was not known how. Vis had been hired to guard ships before, and had helped the crew on some occasions, so he knew his way around a ship fairly well. They both helped Nauto with whatever had to be done, which at that moment was nothing. Silen also knew what had to be done on a ship, for he had once been a pirate. He had climbed up to the crow's nest, keeping a lookout for both land and other ships.

Lamia appeared on deck, and she called the men downstairs into the hold. With the *Ocean's Will* being so large, the hold had four levels. The topmost being the crew's sleeping quarters, and the bottommost being the storage area, holding equipment and animals, the latter needed to feed the crew. The second to last level held the cannons, along with the powder needed to fire them, as well as an armory filled with swords, spears, and bows, all needed to repel any attacks someone had on the ship. The level directly above the cannons was the mess hall, as well as the kitchen, which was where the crew ate and was served, respectively. This is where they were headed now. Silen skillfully climbed down from the masthead and joined the group, following them down into the hold. Ferinus stayed on deck, silently guiding the ship through the water. As Silen reached the mess hall, he saw the now-companions sitting in the center table, of which there were three, all long enough to hold at least twenty people each.

The group were already tucking into their food, which happened to be roast pork. Lamia proved to be a fine cook. Silen went to sit down, and he found himself next to Nauto and across from Atrox. The former seemed to eat huge amounts of food, which was unusual for an elf, while the latter merely picked at his food, taking small bites of the pork and washing it down with a glass of the wine that had been poured into everyone's cups.

There was no conversation going on at the moment, for everyone was starving and focused their attention on the feast, and Silen ate greedily along with the rest of them.

After everyone was done, Nauto spoke up and asked what Lamia knew of Senium Forest, which he had never heard of before, even being a captain of a ship and knowing almost every city and region that Solum contained, having studied many maps of the huge continent.

Upon hearing the name of the destination to which they were traveling to, Atrox seemed to perk up, though no one noticed but Silen, who had been busy trying to catch a glimpse of Atrox's face, to see what he looked like. The hood shifted slightly upon his head, and although the light should have shown upon his face, darkness kept it veiled. Perhaps it was magickal.

Lamia spoke. "The Senium Forest is probably not known to you because it is hidden from every map save one, which is in my possession." She reached into her bag which held her herbs and other magickal items, and retrieved rolled up scroll. She unrolled it and it appeared to be exactly as she said; a map.

Silen had studied many maps himself, and immediately noticed something different about it. For one thing, it seemed that the map was alive on the table. The sea of Orbis appeared to be moving, as if the tides were shown on the map. Many small dots were seen in the sea, and Silen presumed that they were ships. The forests on the map seemed to stand still, moving only when an invisible wind shook them. The volcanoes in the North were bubbling, and one was actually erupting before their eyes. The only thing that was not moving on the map was the mountains, and the words that designated places. The second difference Silen saw was a forest that he had never seen before on any map, which was directly in the center of the volcanoes in the North, and on it were written the words "Senium Forest".

How is that possible? Thought Silen, as he scrutinized the seemingly living map, and looked at the forest that should not have been there.

"This map shows Solum in its current condition." She pointed to a dot close to the centaur region. "This is the ship we are on currently." The dot she pointed to said *Ocean's Will* above it. No other ship had a name.

"Why does only this ship have a name above it?" Silen asked.

"This map shows only the places that I have been to. I have not been on any other ships that are currently in the ocean, since none have names," she answered. "Rest assured, for you may see another dot with a name appear at some other time."

"So you have been to the Senium Forest then? It does have a name on it." Vis pointed out.

Lamia looked confused, and shook her head. "No, I have never been there myself, though this is the first time that I really noticed that a place had a name without me having been there at least once." Vis nodded in understanding and turned his attention back to the map.

"Can you enlighten us about the object we are seeking in the forest?" Lex asked.

"First, a brief historical lesson. Thousands of years ago, the six main races came to Solum. The leaders of each race quickly divided up the land and let the lesser races roam free between each realm after the war with the dragons." Lamia quickly explained. "We do not know where they came from, and why they came here is also a mystery. Many ships have tried to traverse the vast ocean of Praecingo, yet none have succeeded, the ocean being too harsh for any ship to sail on. The Senium Forest is the only piece of land not occupied by any race, despite being in the center of dimidium land. They say a powerful magick protects the forest, so no one can enter."

"How do you expect us to gain access to this forest, then?" Vis asked.

"I have studied almost whole life on the removal of spells, as well as placing them. I believe I can unravel the magick surrounding this forest, and then proceed onward, facing the unknown dangers of the forest. However, all my years of training and studying may all come to naught due to our friend here." She pointed to Atrox, who seemed to be staring intently at the map.

"This did not explain my original question." Lex probed. "What is in the forest that you seek?"

Lamia hesitated before answering. "From what I have studied, I believe that knowledge of the coming to Solum lies in the forest, for it is said that the six rulers of the main races converged there for a meeting. What they discussed is also a mystery, but if there is any chance of discovering the past's secrets, I will take it, no matter what the risk is."

Atrox seemed to start at this, but Silen could not be sure for he only saw a slight movement out of the corner of his eye.

Suddenly a loud roar of warning came from the deck. For a moment, everyone stared at each other, before scrambling to race up the stairs to the deck.

Silen made it up to the deck first, but somehow Atrox was there before him. Silen looked to the wheel, where Ferinus should have been, but he was no longer there.

Silen scanned the deck, and saw Ferinus on the starboard side, peering deep into the water. He walked up to Ferinus, with the others following at a close range behind him. He got to the railing and looked into the depths of the ocean. All he saw was the ceaseless motion of the water.

"What did you see, Ferinus?" Nauto asked hesitantly.

Ferinus looked up and seemed to be in a daze. After a moment, he muttered, "Dragon."

After Ferinus uttered that word, the ocean began to churn. Everyone quickly back away from the deck, unsheathing their weapons. Lex climbed up to the upper deck, stringing her bow as she got to the top of the stairs. Lamia readied her herbs while Nauto got out his sword and a long dagger. Silen took out his own two daggers, both appearing wicked and deadly. Ferinus grasped at the huge mace on his back, and Vis had his two-handed sword in his hands, ready to face anything.

The only one not doing anything was Atrox. He stood in the center of the deck, staring off into the distance.

The water churned faster, until suddenly, a huge, light blue head rose out of the ocean. It was a dragon of the sea; a fully mature one, judging by the size.

Dragons had existed on Solum long before the races came, and after a long war that took place over several decades, the dragons and the races made a treaty to have no further hostilities. The dragon in front of them had a murderous gleam in his eye, and the treaty seemed forgotten.

When his head and neck fully surfaced, he spoke, a deep baritone voice carried his words, and it brought with them the smell of the ocean. "WHO DARES TO TRAVEL THIS OCEAN WITH THE SWORD THAT SLEW SO MANY OF MY KIND?! THE SCENT

PERVADES MY SENSES AND FOGS MY MIND!"

His gaze turned towards Atrox, who did not flinch. "YOU! YOU ARE THE ONE WITH THE LEGENDARY SWORD OF AEVUM! I RECOGNIZE YOU, PUNY HUMAN. YOU WERE THERE THOUSANDS OF YEARS AGO WHEN THE DRAGONS WERE AT WAR WITH THE CURSED PILGRIMS WHO WERE INTENT ON TAKING THIS LAND FOR THEMSELVES!"

Silen covered his ears to ward against the roaring of the dragon, but to no avail, for his voice seemed to go straight into his mind. He could see the others doing the same. The dragon then opened its mouth and sprayed a fine mist over the companions. Everyone fell asleep instantly, save one person.

Atrox.

The dragon's voice pierced the fog of Atrox's mind. He fell to the deck of the ship, holding his head in his hands. His mind was flooded with new yet familiar images. He was able to think once more.

I…………………….................................How……………….. long?……………………….....................It has…………. been………………………...........clouded………………….. ………………………...shrouded from…………………………….my…………………………….. mind……………………………...Am I……………….. ………………………now…………………………….free? Atrox?………………………….......................... …………………………No………………………………….....

Resentful Tide and The Awakening

....
..............................*Ast*...
......*rum*...
.........................*Ast*......*rum*.....................................
....
....
......*Astrum*...
....
...............*I*..
...................*am*...
.............................*ASTRUM!*

    Atrox, actually known as Astrum, clutched his head in seeming agony. He made no noise as he struggled to regain what was lost within him. The veil covering his thoughts and some of his memories was swept away with his will. Lucidity was once more his. He was no longer in a state of a conscious comatose.

    Astrum regared the menacing dragon, ferocity and power emanating from him. Suddenly, with a deep voice rivaling that of the dragon, Astrum spoke. "Yes, Aequor, I was there. I slew thousands of your kind, while saving thousands of more. It was I who persuaded the races to come with a treaty, for I was tired of the constant warfare."

    Astrum stood up, confidence in both his demeanor and stance. He was the master of his fate; no more would some unknown entity shroud his own thoughts from him. He was in control.

    Aequor, the dragon as so named by Astrum, was taken aback. "YOU KNOW MY NAME!? HOW CAN THIS BE?"

    Astrum spoke once again. "I am more than I seem,

serpent of the sea, as you should know by now. I could slay you as well as your brethren who died valiantly but uselessly so many millennia ago, but it would be a waste to do so for you hold so much knowledge of the past. The sword you mentioned is here, sheathed across my back, and it will stay that way, for now. Take heed to my words, Aequor, you will ferry our ship to the volcanic lands held by the dimidium, so we may reach the Senium Forest. After doing so, you would be wise to tell your brethren in the sea of us, so that we may never again be molested by sea dragons and the like."

Aequor nodded his giant head, and hissed, "IT SHALL BE DONE." He looked at Astrum vengefully, and then slipped back under the ocean, leaving only a small ripple in his wake.

Astrum's memories returned, though he still did not feel complete. Something was still missing. He let it slip from his mind, however, and he looked towards his companions. He waved his hand above them, and one by one, they awoke. They all stood up and gawked at Astrum in awe. He had apparently somehow bartered with the dragon, though since they were asleep, they knew not how.

The boat soon began to travel noticeably faster. The dragon towed their boat towards their destination, traveling as fast as a sea dragon could, desperate to be away from that man as soon as possible.

Chapter 4

Preserved Darkness

Two beings unlike any other were sitting down, playing a game of chess. One was huge, his belly nearly touching the table, though he was sitting fairly far back. His eyes flashed orange as he closely observed the chessboard. The other being was far slimmer than her companion, though both were unbelievable huge, as in any human would think they were gods, as they easily were larger than the whole land of Solum. The slim being was a female, and wore little in the way of clothing. Her eyes glowed with a deep blue.

Their chessboard was unlike any other, for it had not one tier, but five, each being immense. Instead of the pieces being one of six different ones, there were many different types of pieces. Their were ones shaped like dimidium dominating the first board, the lowest one, as centaur shaped pieces dominated the second, and humans did the third, the elves the fourth, and the dwarves and gnome shaped pieces did the fifth. Many other differently shaped pieces were strewn randomly about the boards, having no order, but some being huge in their own right.

The beings moved these pieces according to where they were ordered that they should be moved to. These immense-beyond-imagination beings took the small pieces in between their fingers and moved them across the also immense-beyond-imagination chessboard.

There were several of pieces they never touched, however. One in particular was shaped like a human, and it shone a deep green. This piece moved of its own accord, with no volition from the two beings. It moved with impunity, knocking over other pieces at times, and moving some of its own. At the moment, it was moving with seven other pieces on the second tier, moving to the first.

The beings watched with interest at the "Shining piece of life", or "Lucidus" piece (this was the beings' name for that piece that they could not touch.) They had not seen it ever move with so many other pieces. It had been traveling with the dimidium piece for some time, but it had never moved with more than three at a time. A part of the small piece of cloth that had been covering the piece was suddenly ripped off of it by some unknown force. The being the piece represented had regained some control.

The beings stopped moving their pieces and focused their full attention on that single piece that was unlike any other. It had just moved down the hole that was in the middle of each tier of the second tier, and gone onto the first tier, moving up the board. One of the pieces, a large blue piece shaped like a dragon, stopped moving with the group and headed back up to the second tier.

When the group reached the spot C3 on the first tier of the chessboard, the beings appeared slightly discomforted. No piece had ever been on C3, for the being purposefully moved pieces around that spot, for that was where the greatest evil in existence lay dormant, marked by a pure black piece also shaped like a human, which, coincidentally, was another piece they never touched.

The beings soon to become worried as the pieces came closer together. They quickly moved twenty dimidium pieces to intercept the group, along with a large red piece shaped like a dragon, just in case. The evil must not be awakened.

Nauto had reluctantly left his boat, and Ferinus had gone also, for Atrox had hidden the boat from view, making it completely invisible, and rendering any guard on it useless. They had proceeded on, after Lex stocked up arrows from the ship's armory, and had also taken a sword.

The group had trekked past three volcanoes before they sighted the forest from atop of the dormant third volcano. The forest below them seemed as if it was in an eternal night, for it had a darkness surrounding it, along with a thick mist that was mocking the midday sun.

They reached the base of the volcano, but still had to make it through a long plain of blackened rock. Nauto gazed ahead. Some distance away he saw dimidium soldiers, seemingly patrolling the forest. As the Nauto and the companions made it closer to the group, the dragon-men stopped marching, and stood their ground at one spot, right in the path of the group.

When the group approached the soldiers, one spoke up, "What is your purpose here? This forest is off-limits to every being, for it is too dangerous to enter."

Nauto was amazed again, for this dimidium was like Vis; he did not slur the "s" when he spoke. Nauto stepped up and spoke. "We were going to go into the forest, actually, for one of our number has read that there is a piece of history here dating from just after the main races landed here. We are going into the forest to see if this is true, and if it is, learn from it."

The dimidium snorted and walked over to them. "Yes, there IS a piece of history in this forest, but it is not what you think it is. It is of the greatest of evils, never to be removed from the forest, which is its prison. That is why it is omitted from maps. It is too evil to even think about." he scoffed, and continued, "There has to be a new patrol around this forest every year, for past that amount of time, people go mad from the darkness emanating from this place. Turn back now, or you will die, either from us or the evil that lay dormant."

As Nauto pondered what the dimidium had told them of the forest, he turned to his companions, more specifically Lamia. "Lamia, did you know that this thing inside this forest was evil?"

Lamia slowly shook her head, her eyes wide. Nauto nodded to her, and then turned back to the soldiers. "We will leave this place now, thank you for saving us from what could have been a terrible fate."

The dimidium nodded. "You are welcome, now please depart, and go in--" whatever the dimidium was going to say next was cut off from a load roar that echoed against the volcanoes. A massive shadow was cast over the group. A flapping of gigantic wings could be heard, and the companions peered upward.

Above them was a dragon even bigger than the one that was in the ocean. This huge, red monstrosity landed some distance away from the group, but the distance did nothing to diminish its size. It stood to be higher than the trees of the forest, and the wings were the double the size of the body. Its red scales glinted in the sunlight.

The dragon regarded the group with contempt. The dragon sniffed once, and then turned its baleful eyes on Atrox.

"YOU! YOU ARE THE ONE CARRYING THE SWORD AEVUM, THE SWORD OF LIFE, THOUGH ALSO OF DEATH. YOU ARE THE ONE WHO MY COUSIN FROM THE SEA SUMMONED ME FOR. YOU WILL DIE FOR YOUR FOLLY, PUNY INSECT!" The dragon's voice was as loud as the one from the sea, but since it was some distance away, the companions could hear and understand what it said. They looked at Atrox, who had unsheathed his blade, apparently prepared to fight this dragon.

"No! You cannot face that dragon, Atrox! It is too

large, too powerful!" Lamia bellowed.

Atrox turned to face her, and the rest of the group, as well as the dimidium soldiers. He then spoke, a resounding voice that had not been heard by human, elf, or dimidium ears for thousands upon thousands of years.

"Go. Go into the forest. I will meet with you shortly. It is your only chance. I will be fine," his deep voice commanded. The shock of his voice preceded the shock of what he was telling them to do. Silen and Vis fled into the forest, closely followed by Lex and Lamia, and then the dimidium soldiers and the rest of the group. Nauto stayed behind for a second longer, looking at Atrox.

"Atrox, please, no matter how powerful you may be, you will not--" Nauto started to plead.

"My name is not Atrox. It is Astrum, and I am immortal. Go now, or I will be forced to take you into the forest," Atrox, or Astrum, rather, commanded.

"But…" Nauto started, but was cut off when Astrum waved his hand, and the next thing Nauto saw was a white light, then he was standing next to his companions in the forest.

Nauto sighed. He looked at Astrum, hoping desperately he could kill the monstrosity.

Cinis, the dragon, snorted in laughter. The huge red dragon had lived far too long to be scared of a human with a special sword.

"YOU DARE CHALLENGE ME ALONE,

HUMAN? THEN AGAIN, YOU HAD NO CHANCE EVEN WITH YOUR COMPANIONS, SO YOUR LIFE WAS FORFEIT, NO MATTER WHAT!" Still laughing, Cinis let loose a great stream of fire from his mouth. It soared high into the sky before dissipating.

Cinis was too far away to smell the human, so he could not sense his true nature. He was not daunted, like his cousin of the sea, by this man.

Cinis let loose his most terrifying roar, and then started to run towards the human at a frightening speed. The human, much to the dragon's shock, started to run also! Cinis looked at the human in amusement, thinking of the death wish this insect must have. Cinis soon realized however, that as the two grew closer, that the human was running twice as fast as himself!

The worm of uncertainty made its way into Cinis's thoughts. The human could not be faster than a dragon, could he? Cinis brushed the thought aside, for it did not matter to him. No matter how fast this human appeared to be, his death would come shortly.

Just as the two were about to collide, the human jumped into the air, landing on Cinis' back. Cinis blinked in surprise as the human buried his sword into his back, where the hardest of Cinis' scales were.

Cinis roared in pain and anger. He stopped running and turned his neck and head towards the human. He had taken out the sword and was now running at an inhuman speed towards his head. The dragon let loose a burst of fire towards the human, watching in satisfaction as the human was engulfed.

He looked at the spot where the human was when the flames cleared. There was no sign of him, not even ashes. *My fire consumed him, leaving no trace.* Cinis arrogantly thought. He turned his head around and reared back in bewilderment as he saw the human floating at the height of his head.

Cinis breathed out fire again, letting the flame wash over the human for several moments, thoroughly bathing him. He stopped flame and was astonished to see the human still there, unscathed!

Cinis studied the human intently. Lowering his voice to a decibel low enough for the human to hear without deafening him, he asked, "What are you, human? No being can withstand my fire, nor order a dragon of the seas without feeling his fury."

The human answered, his voice revealing no emotion, though Cinis had expected fear to put a quiver in the man's voice. "What I am is of no importance to you, for whether I tell you or not, you will die."

"SUCH INSOLENCE, THE LIKES OF WHICH I HAVE NEVER KNOWN! You claim much in that one sentence, human, but you are wrong. Only one of us will die, and it will be you. I have lived for hundreds upon hundreds of years, and I plan to live for many more. No human can hope to best me, for they cannot experience the world in the short eighty years they live." Cinis studied the human closely.

"Aye, dragons live longer than humans, but it is possible for one such to kill you, Cinis." The human gazed back at Cinis, staring him straight in the eye.

"WHAT!? NO MORTAL KNOWS MY NAME!" Cinis reared back once more.

"It is a good thing I am not mortal then, is it not?" The human pulled back his hood, revealing his features.

His short and messy blond hair, along with his sharp features, did little to detract attention to his eyes. Cinis stared deeply into those eyes, and as he looked into them he saw the bright green irises expand until they filled the corners of his eyes. Green sparks jumped up from his eyes, and as Cinis stood transfixed, the sparks leapt out and struck the dragon.

What power! What is this human?! Cinis thought as the sparks hit him with such force to throw him back hundreds of feet. He slid across the landscape, leaving great jagged marks in the ground from his scales and spikes. It did more for his anger than it did for his pain, yet as he stood up again, he started to feel something that he had never felt before.

Fear.

Pure, unadulterated terror that prevented him from thinking clearly, and indeed, from thinking at all. This fear was so much that Cinis was reduced to little more than a dog, albeit a dog with very sharp claws and huge wings.

The human started to run towards Cinis, but Cinis did not care, for he had no more feelings anymore, due to his lack of thought that the fear had brought him. Cinis looked towards the human with no interest. The human then sprung up and brought the green sword down towards Cinis's head. They pierced his scales and were driven down through his skull, and then the dragon absolutely was not able to think anymore.

His giant body fell to the ground, decaying rapidly. Within a minute, there was nothing left of the dragon.

The beings snorted in annoyance as the chess piece shaped like a dragon disintegrated. The dimidium pieces, the beings noticed, did nothing to stop the group, and indeed they started to run away from the group as Lucidus moved towards them.

Their cowardice angered the beings, and they moved them away from the "Shining piece of life", save one, who they could not move, for it was too close to "Lucidus".

The companions and the dimidium soldiers stared at Astrum in disbelief. He had felled a dragon that was larger than all of them put together twice, and he did not even have one scratch to show for it, not one burn mark on his skin.

As Astrum walked closer to the group, Nauto heard murmurings of fear behind him, and soon heard the sound of running feet as the dimidium soldiers ran away from this dragon-killer.

The dimidium who had talked to the group remained, and he walked up to Nauto. His red scales glinted in the sun. "Elf, I beseech you, let me travel with you to the center of the forest. This *thing* who travels with you is more than a match for the evil that lies sleeping in this forest, and so if he destroys it, we can stop patrolling this cursed place. I have a map that shows the only path to the center of the forest, and it will be of great use to you." He took out a parchment as he spoke, and unraveled it to show a map of the forest.

Nauto studied the map with interest, and spoke to the dimidium, "All right, we will rid the forest of this evil, or, rather, Astrum will." He pointed to the man who was walking closer to them. "Perhaps we can still learn a bit of history in doing so, also, as was our original intent."

The dimidium looked relieved beyond measure at Nauto's words. "My name is Munus, and I am a dimidium officer." They shook hands, and noticed that Astrum was upon them.

Astrum's face had an ageless quality about it, like that of the elves. He appeared to be young, perhaps in his twenties, in human years. He held his sword in one hand, despite it being almost as long as he was tall. He had light blond hair that was cut short and messy.

He had both the qualities of a king and a feral animal, making him seem composed yet fierce. The most defining feature, however, was his bright green eyes that, when Nauto stared into them, seemed to contain the whole universe, as he could see stars in his pupils, though that seemed impossible.

He appeared both human and yet also the furthest thing from it, even more so than he, an elf, or Vis or Ferinus.

Nauto could not find the words for a moment, then simply said, "Thank you."

Astrum sheathed his sword and nodded. He said nothing, mute once more. Nauto stared into his eyes again, and then turned around, facing the forest. He started to walk slowly to the center, followed by the others, including Munus.

Lamia shook her head. The closer she got to the center of the forest, the dizzier she felt. She followed the companions from behind, and scanned the forest warily. She could sense dark energies all around, but saw nothing but twisted trees. She gazed ahead to look at Astrum at the front of the group. His stride was like that of a king, long and purposeful, never faltering. Perhaps he was a king. How would anyone know? He had only spoken serveral of times, and what he said never contained pieces of his own life.

Lamia was jealous of Astrum. He was a much more accomplished magick-user than she would ever be, although she spent all of her life perfecting her spells. When they had gotten to the magickal barrier that surrounded the forest, he had simply waved his hand, and it dissipated. All of her hard work, for nothing. It did not even seem as though the spell had depleted his energy at all, he just kept walking forward, none the worse for wear.

Lamia sighed, and then looked to the next person in the group, who followed closely behind Astrum. It was Nauto, and he was glancing all around, his rapier in his right hand and a dagger in his left. Nothing would escape his elf eyes, though Lamia saw little point in his cautiousness, as Astrum would surely take care of any foul beast that might come upon them. Though the forest was oddly silent, and nothing stirred save for the group of companions. Lamia had not been to many dark forests, but she was sure that at least some animals would inhabit the trees.

The next person in the group was Vis. He also had his weapon drawn, and held it so that the point of the sword was straight up. Though the weapon was huge, he held easily, as though it were a feather. The wings on his back shuddered slightly with each step. His green scales were muted, as no sunlight passed through the darkened canopy. It might be night by now anyway, for all she knew.

After Vis came Silen. He held no weapons in his hands, but being a thief, and therefore a master of sleight of hand, he could most likely pull them out in a blink of an eye. Lamia was still angry at him for stealing her money, but without him, she would have never met Nauto and everyone else, so he did not deserve her wrath. His footsteps made no sounds, unlike the rest of the group, with the exception of Astrum.

Lex followed Silen. She had her bow how, an arrow nocked, ready to fire. Her chain mail clinked with every step. Lamia did not know what to make of her. She had not made any complaints when the group took her with them, and she had not tried attacking Astrum again either. She would have to get better acquainted with Lex to learn more about her, as well as to be closer friends with the only other female on this voyage.

Ferinus lumbered through the forest, breaking tree branches in his way with ease. A huge mace rested on his back, ready to be taken out and break not only bones, but bodies. Lamia did not know what to make of him, either. What dark sorcery could have brought about such a creature? Munus was also looking at Ferinus, as well as Astrum. The dimidium did not know what to make of this motley group, but he followed them all the same, eager to see the end of the supposed "evil" in the middle of the forest. Not that Lamia did not believe there was something like that in the forest, for the trees themselves seemed to resonate with evil, but just that the sorcery that enthralled the forest might not be evil, it might have just had unfortunate consequences, as most magick did, which is why many people fear it.

Suddenly, Astrum held up his hand, and the group halted. He cocked his head to the left, and then put his hand on his sword strapped to his back. The rest of the group, those who did not have their weapons at the ready, proceeded to take them out in anticipation. Silen took out two wicked looking daggers, and reversed them in his hands, so they pointed backwards. Ferinus took off the huge mace he wore on his back, and held it in both hands. Munus unsheathed a short sword and grabbed his shield from his back. Lamia already had her weapon out, a long staff. Some might say it was a bad choice of weaponry, but Lamia knew better, as it enhanced her magick and she was able to wield it with deadly efficiency if she could not cast spells.

Astrum then unsheathed the sword he held his hand on, and pointed it out in front of him. He walked forward slowly, while the rest of the group followed. He cut through a tree branch in his way, and the rest of the tree shimmered, then disappeared without a trace. Ahead of him, now that the tree was not blocking the way, Lamia could see a clearing. As she walked into the clearing last, she could see a block of stone, and a body lay upon it. It was a man. His hair was jet black, and was very long. His face, though he lay asleep, seemed to be filled with hate. He wore a kingly robe, though instead of royal colors, such as purple or blue, it was black as night. Nothing else lay in the clearing. Astrum approached the man cautiously. Everyone else stayed far back, letting Astrum do whatever it was he needed to do.

"I did not think the evil would just be a mere man." Munus whispered, with a touch of relief in his voice.

"Looks can be deceiving." Silen whispered back.

Astrum reached the man, and looked down upon him. After a long moment, Astrum sheathed his sword, and walked back towards the group. When he reached them, he spoke. "Do not approach this body; he is not to be tampered with. He must lie here, asleep, so that his plague will not reach the rest of Solum."

The group did not question him, save one. "Why not just kill him? You surely can do so," Munus retorted. "In fact, I could kill him. He is but a mere man, and a sleeping one at that."

Astrum regarded Munus with a raised eyebrow. "Do you not believe me?" his voice held no emotion, though it seemed as though he was daring Munus to disregard his words. Munus gazed up at him, then shook his head and turned around. The rest of the group walked out, Astrum taking the lead again, and Munus at the end.

As Lamia passed into the trees, she heard Munus laughing. She turned around and looked at him. He opened his mouth and breathed fire into the trees. The forest caught aflame almost instantly. He then ran to the sleeping figure, sword in hand. Astrum ran to the flame barrier, and put it out instantly, but he was too late.

Munus smiled, and then cut his hand with his sword. He held it over the man's face, and blood dropped into his mouth. "My master will awaken once more, and rule the land. There is nothing you can do to stop him!" Munus then kneeled down before his "master".

"I thought you wanted him killed!" Lamia shouted.

Munus replied without looking back, focused on the sleeping man. "No, it was a simple façade. This man is the embodiment of darkness, and my people worship him. We have never been able to gain entry into the forest, however, until you came along."

The man on the stone block started to shake. "It has begun! The reign of the master of darkness shall soon begin!" Munus laughed maniacally. The man then opened his eyes, and let out a long laugh. He sat up, and looked down at Munus where he kneeled. His eyes flashed bright red in delight.

"I have awoken! I thank you, faithful servant. I see that thy dimidium have not forgotten their true master, Umbra! Hand me thy sword, servant; I am in need of more blood," the man spoke, his voice filled with malicious intent, yet his speech was old fashioned and he had a strange accent. Munus held his sword towards the man, and he grasped it with his right hand, still smiling. He waved his hand over it, and it grew in size, and changed color from one of grey to pitch black. He then swung the blade, severing the head of the dimidium officer in one blow. Blood spurted from the decapitated body, and the man stepped into the flow and bathed in it.

Umbra beheld the head with glee, then smoothed back his hair and regarded the rest of the group. He raised his eyebrow at Silen, and also at Lamia, at which she started. Then he laid his eyes upon Astrum, raised both eyebrows.

"Ah…so, Astrum, you have come to free me then. I knew no other besides one of us could break the barrier of the forest," Astrum looked at Umbra with pure confusion, and his sword lowered a little. "Oh? Do you not remember me? It is for the best, I suppose, as those were *very* painful times; for you, that is," his smile grew wider, and he strode towards the group. Astrum lifted his sword again, the look of confusion gone, replaced with one of determination.

Umbra laughed and ran towards Astrum, raising his sword as he ran. When he reached Astrum, he swung his sword downwards, and Astrum blocked it with his own. Astrum pushed Umbra's sword back and swung his in a horizontal swipe. Umbra jumped back and Astrum followed. This all happened within a matter of a few seconds, as their movements were almost too fast to perceive.

None of the members of the group wanted to interfere, for if they did, they knew it would mean death. They held back and watched the battle with amazement. The intricate movements of the swords of Astrum and Umbra were furiously quick. Such a battle could only be fought with hundreds of years of battle experience, as both of them surely had.

After a few more moments of battling, Umbra jumped back onto the stone where he once laid, his face changed from one of glee to rage. Astrum looked at Umbra, his face still resolute. Umbra then spoke.

"I see you have surpassed even me in

swordsmanship, though we once had our roles reversed, long ago. No matter, you will not interrupt the plans I have been making in the past millennia. This land will face my wrath, and war will be unavoidable," Umbra stated. "And to make this fate unavoidable, I now use the same curse on you that you used to defeat me long ago." He held out his hand, and muttered a few words under his breath. The air crackled with power, and a beam of sable light shot out from Umbra's hand and into Astrum's chest. Astrum dropped his sword and fell to his knees. He let out a gasp, and then fell to the ground.

Umbra laughed, and then looked to the sky. He dropped his sword, which turned back into what it was before he held it. He grew huge, black, scaled wings, and flew off to the sky, then headed in a northeast direction after reaching the tops of the trees. Umbra was gone from sight after a few seconds.

The forest around the group turned less malevolent as Umbra left, and the trees became untwisted, with green leaves replacing the black ones. The forest had been freed from its evil inhabitant, and so life once again flourished immediately.

The group stared in horror at Astrum, who was still lying on the ground. Astrum then groaned, and got up. He picked up his sword and sheathed it. He looked around, but, seeing no trace of Umbra, walked towards the group.

Lamia looked at Astrum, and realized something peculiar had happened to him. She no longer felt an aura of magick emanating from Astrum, and proceeded to tell him so. To test this, Astrum tried making fire appear out of thin air. He waved his hand and held it up to the sky. Everyone waited expectantly. Nothing happened. He stared at his hand and shook it, as if trying to make it work.

Astrum looked at the group, and simply stated, "Well, that cannot be good.

Chapter 5

Cold Desolation

The group, led by Nauto now, had left the forest, and was now on the ship. Astrum's invisibility enchantment was still in effect, but Lamia was able to dispel it with little difficulty. Astrum still had superb strength and speed, as he had tested before they left the forest, but that had been no magick, just practice and experience. He suffered no injuries, no maladies, neither physical nor mental.

Though he had lost his magick, he had opened up more to the group, rather than playing mute, like he had before. It was the complete opposite reaction Lex had been expecting. Her hatred for him dimmed as she realized that he was not the soulless killing monster like she had thought of him as before. He was actually very witty, and always seemed to know what to say.

Lex sighed as she looked over the deck railing. She had taken off her armor, and had on a simple dress that Lamia had given her. She felt naked without her armor and, especially, her bow. But Lamia had convinced her to not be so cautious, as she was among friends. The past couple of days being out to sea, and then with the incident at the forest, she realized that these people truly wanted to know her, and life on the ship was joyful.

That is not to say that everyone felt totally at ease on the ship, what with Umbra out and about, and with Astrum's power gone. Astrum, Nauto, Silen, and Vis were in Nauto's cabin, deciding what they should do next. Ferinus stood at the wheel, and Lamia was sleeping in her room. Lex decided to join the men in the cabin, to see what their thoughts were. She nodded to Ferinus as she passed by him, and made her way to the cabin. It took several moments, as the ship was fairly large, but when she did get there, she knocked on the door three times, and waited. The door opened wide and Vis stood in the doorway.

"Come in," he said. Lex nodded and did as he offered.

She looked around in amazement. She had never been in a captain's quarters before, on this ship nor any other. Treasures of all types were stacked high, some stacks reaching the ceiling. Gold glittered everywhere, as well as colorful glows from gemstones. Books of every shape and size were strewn about the cabin as well. She looked at the table where Silen, Astrum, and Nauto were standing at, inspecting maps of Solum.

She walked to the table, and stood in an empty spot. Vis followed her and did the same. The map they were currently looking at was Lamia's, as only certain things were named, and Lex could see clouds passing over the map, as if it were a miniature world in itself. The table was silent, and so Lex spent her time looking over the map.

It was strange seeing Solum from a high viewpoint such as this, it was as if she were a bird, or, due to recent events, a dragon. Lex could not imagine herself to be a fearsome beast with magickal powers, so she stuck with feeling like a bird.

Nauto then spoke up. "So," he started, "Any ideas on where Umbra may be found?"

Astrum replied with, "Even if we find him, how are we to defeat him? I have lost my magick, and with him being just as powerful as I was, I doubt anyone could defeat him."

Silen stood there silently contemplating the map, a thoughtful expression on his face. "Well, Umbra said that you had used the curse on him first, so if you could remember the curse, perhaps Lamia could cast it?" Astrum nodded for a moment, but then shook his head.

"I do not remember the curse, and I do not remember him, though he said we knew each other long ago," Astrum answered with a sigh. Silen regarded Astrum silently, and then looked back down at the map.

Lex suddenly remembered something else Umbra had said. She stared at Vis suspiciously, and then spoke up. "Umbra also mentioned that the dimidium did not forget their master. Do you know anything of this, Vis?"

Vis looked back at her with surprise. He thought for a moment, and then replied. "I can see how you would think that I would bow down before Umbra, but this is not true. It is true that I knew of this master of the dimidium, because in the city I grew up in, there was a temple dedicated to him. Other than that, I know nothing of him. I have been away from my people twenty years, and no longer feel like one of them."

Astrum nodded. "Yes, it is true. Some jobs we had, being mercenaries, were to guard caravans, and they were sometimes attacked. Vis and I slew many dimidium who tried to raid our employer's caravan."

Lex nodded, but then thought of something else. "Vis, where was it you grew up?"

Vis looked at her confusedly. "Incendia quod Inculta, why?"

She gave a knowing smile, and then stated with bravado, "Well, we know where he is then, correct? He would want to go where he would be worshipped, right?"

Lex looked around at the group, and felt satisfaction as she saw them all nodding slowly. "Yes, that seems to be it," Nauto said. "But we are only on square two now, for we still have no way to defeat him."

Silen spoke up. "Just a question; why are we bothering to try and defeat him at all?"

Astrum had an answer. "He stated he was going to start a war. Is that not reason enough?"

Lex added, "Yes, and do not you feel as though it is our fault, at least in part?"

Silen raised his hands to appease them, and then said, "All right, all right, fair enough, I just wanted good reason to go after an immensely powerful and dark being, is all. But still the question remains; how are we to defeat him? We have no armies to match his own, as we are as motley a group as any other out there, but we have no connections with any kings, none that I know of anyway."

Nauto then spoke. "Well, I know no kings, but I do remember stories of a being of vast power in the elven forest of Altus, a forest where trees grow to become immense mountains in their own right. It is said that this being will bring an end to plague when the time comes. Perhaps this is the time?"

Everyone nodded in agreement, and Nauto went outside to give Ferinus a new heading. Soon they were on their way. It was a small hope, no more than a theory and a legend, but it was all they had.

Umbra loved the feeling of freedom, the feeling of the wind beneath his wings. He flew on to the city of the dimidium, Incendia quod Inculta. There, in the city that was between the volcanoes and the desert, was a temple devoted to the dark, devoted to him. He gazed up at the stars, their white light twinkling on the world below. Umbra scoffed, and waved his hand. The stars' light became obscured by great clouds.

Much better, Umbra thought to himself. He looked down at the barren landscape, and then forward. There lay the city, a large wall encircling its entirety. One half lay in the desert, with a large river flowing through it, the only river in the entire desert. The other half lay in the volcanic side, and also had a river flowing through it, though this one was of lava. Where the two rivers met in the walled city was where his temple lay. He could already see its black spire piercing the sky. The temple was as large as a citadel, and appeared as such as well. It was a blackened metal monstrosity to all but Umbra's eyes, who saw it as his kingdom and home.

When he passed over the wall of the city, he peered downward to see the dimidium looking up at him and pointing. Someone screamed, "HE IS BACK!"

Umbra laughed and replied, "YES, I HAVE RETURNED FROM MY SLUMBER. COME, MY FAITHFUL, TO MY TEMPLE!" he flew into the spire, ignoring the stairs that the cooled lava made. His wings folded back into him, and he walked calmly to his throne that had lain dormant for so many years. He sat down, and then waited.

Soon, it seemed as though the whole city poured into the black halls of his temple, though it was more akin to a castle. Dimidium of every color swarmed in, and sat down in the black pews, though most had to stand. The temple hall was full of dimidium, each excited to see their master awakened. Umbra raised his hands and silenced the din instantly, save for one dimidium.

"Let me through! I need to get to him!" the blue-scaled dimidium shouted. He held a bundle of cloth in his hands, and it seemed very heavy. Everyone was so intent upon their master that no one stepped aside, no matter how much he pushed and shoved.

Umbra looked at this dimidium with a bemused smile upon his face. "Let him through," Umbra commanded. "I wish to see what it is he has for me."

the crowd parted instantly. Panting, the blue dimidium walked to Umbra, bundle held tightly.

When he got to the throne, he knelt down and offered up the bundle to Umbra, who took it. The blue dimidium looked up expectantly. Umbra unwrapped the cloth, and threw it aside. Inside there was a sword. Its long, black blade curved fiercely into the sky as Umbra held it up. A smile lit upon his face as his red eyes gazed upon his sword, named Diabolus.

"And now," Umbra rejoiced, "my reign begins!" The dimidium crowd cheered, and their cacophony shook the temple walls.

Umbra smiled as the dimidium prepared to make war on the world of those who wronged him, namely, the elves and Astrum. *Though,* he thought, *it will not be enough with just one race, I must recruit more. The humans may yield to my rule, though that is doubtful, after being neighbors to the elves for so long. Gnomes do not make good soldiers, so that only leaves the centaur and dwarves.* Umbra smiled, and though he seemed happy, he raged inside. All the anger and frustration pent up for thousands of years was difficult to keep caged in, but he knew he could not take over the land without armies, for his opposite, Lumen, would keep his power in check, creating balance. That would do no good, for Umbra wanted destruction, not a stalemate.

Chapter 6

Meditative Battle

Astrum left the Nauto's cabin as the group started to talk of dinner. They were such a carefree group; the threat of annihilation by an evil and wrathful being hanging over their heads, and here they were talking of whether they should have pork or bird. He walked to the middle of the deck and sat down, legs crossed, hands on his knees. He meditated like this every so often, though the ritual consisted of far more than sitting and mulling over his thoughts.

He opened his eyes and they blazed with verdant ferocity. He sprung from the ground, drawing his sword midair. As he came down, he performed a vertical slice with his sword, effectively chopping his imaginary foe in half. This process cleared his mind; he would think of all his troubles, and then imagined that they all attacked him simultaneously and he would have to fight them off.

Astrum brought his sword back up and swung around, bringing his foot up as he spun, kicking one of the imaginary foes in the face. He came around fully and brought his sword down on its neck. He stabbed forward, and then jumped back, spun around, and pivoted midair. He brought his sword down on an enemy's shield, cleaving it in two. He tilted backward, avoiding the enemy's sword whose shield he ruined, and, as he leaned back, he thrust his sword behind, over his face, and stabbed an enemy in his. He brought his sword forward again, and caught the foe's sword as he recovered from his slash and swung his sword in the opposite direction. His sword met Astrum's, and it was forced from his hand as Astrum's sword went through half the blade and stopped. Astrum, the enemy's sword stuck on his own, brought his sword upward, so the foe's own sword went up into his head from his chin. Astrum released his blade from the enemy's, grabbed that enemy's sword again, and threw the imaginary sword at another foe, where it stuck in his chest. Two enemies converged upon him at once, and brought their swords upon his head. He swung his sword up and knocked both of their swords away, and then Astrum spun around and slit both of their throats.

Astrum stood up and sheathed his sword. He surveyed his surrounding again, and the bodies of his imaginary foes disappeared, evaporating into thin air. He nodded once in satisfaction, his mind cleared. Astrum looked towards the crew's quarter's stairs, and

Meditative Battle

saw Lamia looking at him, her expression one of alarm. He turned around to the captain's quarters, and saw that everyone else had similar expressions on their faces. Astrum looked back at them, then at Lamia, shrugged his shoulders, and asked, "What?"

Nauto regained composure first, and meekly mumbled, "We are having pork."

Astrum nodded, and then made his way down to the mess hall. As he passed by Lamia he winked at her. She still stood there, confused.

Dinner was finished, and they sat there silently. Silen picked his teeth with a small dagger he had, and Nauto brought the tableware to the kitchen. He washed everything that needed it, and then returned to his spot. Before he could actually sit down though, the ship shuddered to a stop, and everyone stood up, and looked around, confused. A wrathful roar was heard from the deck; it sounded like Ferinus. Everyone rushed up the stairs, Nauto taking the lead, Astrum at the back.

When Nauto reached the top of the stairs, he saw Ferinus standing in the middle of the deck, staring angrily at Nauto. He had thrown the anchor overboard.

"Where is that hooded man?!" Ferinus roared.

Everyone made it to the deck, and when Astrum came out, Ferinus pointed one claw at him in accusation. "You! I had not remembered who it was who knocked me unconscious some time ago, but now I remember! It was you! I demand the right to fight you, for you paid me great dishonor!"

Nauto spoke, soothingly telling Ferinus to calm down. Ferinus would have none of it, and before the two started to fight themselves, Astrum stepped up.

"Enough," he commanded. "I will combat you, Ferinus, so that you may regain your honor. Know, however, that if you lose, you may not challenge me again; you are given this one chance."

Ferinus calmed down a bit, then nodded his head; he was beastly but he knew of honor and respect. He took his mace, and threw it to the side. It hit the deck and cracked the planks it landed on. Astrum, seeing this, took off his sword, and handed it to Silen, who was closest. He also removed his armor, which he handed to Lex, who was second-closest to him.

He stretched his arms and legs, then hopped a couple of times, readying for the fight. Ferinus snorted, and cracked his knuckles, each making a very loud noise. Everyone else went to the upper deck, at the prow of the ship, above the crew's quarters, and looked down upon Astrum and Ferinus.

Surprisingly, Astrum ran towards Ferinus first. Ferinus laughed gruffly, and charged at Astrum, head down, horns pointed forward. As the two were about to collide, Astrum jumped up over Ferinus, landed on his back, jumped off, and did a front flip. He landed on the ground gracefully. Ferinus stumbled as Astrum jumped off his back, but corrected himself almost immediately. He turned around and snorted again, this time in rage. Ferinus charged again, but this time Astrum stood still. When it seemed inevitable that Astrum would be gored by his horns, the group looked away. The only ones still watching were Nauto and Vis, Nauto because he knew

Meditative Battle

Ferinus would not kill Astrum, and Vis because he knew that Astrum would not be beaten as easily as that.

Vis was correct. Astrum grabbed the charging Ferinus by his horns, and forced his head down. His head stopped moving forward, but the rest of his body did not. His body flew up into the air, and it seemed as though it would land on Astrum, crushing him.

In fact, it did land on Astrum, but it was far from crushing him. Astrum had let go of Ferinus' horns, and caught his flipped body. He held Ferinus for a second, and then threw him to the ground. Ferinus landed with a loud *crack* as the deck's wooden floor broke slightly. Ferinus sat up, shaking his head, dazed from the drop. Astrum looked at Ferinus, awaiting his next move. There was none, however, as Ferinus stood up and held out his hand without a word. Astrum stared at it, and then shook hands with him.

Nauto and Vis made their way down to the deck and applauded the two. The Lamia also clapped, but Silen and Lex could not do so very well, as they were still holding Astrum's gear. Astrum relieved the two of their burden, and put everything back on. Ferinus grunted, and then went to the side of the ship. He brought the anchor he had dropped back onto the ship, and went back to the wheel, fixing their course to reach the elven lands.

Fighting Ferinus had not been a good idea, Astrum now thought, as the others now wanted to fight him, to see if anyone could match him in combat. He sighed, exasperated with the pleading voices of his companions. Finally, he raised his hands in defeat.

"Fine," he relented, "I will fight you each. Happy?" The expressions on their faces lit with joy. The only one who did not care was Vis, as he and Astrum had sparred before, and Vis had lost many a time, every time they had done so, in fact. Vis did not think the others knew what they were in for.

First to go was Nauto. He claimed the right to as he was captain of the ship. The group had relented, walked to where they were when Ferinus and Astrum had fought, and the combatants stood facing each other, Astrum with his sword drawn, Nauto with his rapier and a long dagger.

"Before we begin," Nauto started, "I have a question; why do you wear armor, Astrum? Surely you have no need for it?"

Astrum chuckled, and then answered, "I have no idea. I have worn it for as long as I can remember, although in the terms of my life I do not think I remember much. Aesthetics?" he shrugged.

His question answered, however poorly, Nauto bent slightly into a combat stance, and Astrum did the same. They stood for a long time, watching each other. Nauto made the first move.

Nauto went on the offensive as he twirled around, full of elven grace, and swung both his weapons at Astrum, who blocked it as easily as if he was swatting away a fly. Undeterred, Nauto jumped back, and stabbed at Astrum's abdomen with his rapier, while reversing his dagger in his hand. Astrum leaned forward, bring his stomach back to avoid Nauto's sword, and then tilted his head to the side as Nauto brought his dagger down in a diagonal slash. Astrum then swung his sword upward with both hands, and Nauto had to retreat. This retreat was unsuccessful; he stepped backwards and promptly fell down on his backside, due to the change in the incline of the ship's deck as a large wave hit the front of the boat. Though he was practiced on a ship, performing a backward leap such as that just as a wave hits would cause many to falter. Taking advantage of this, Astrum brought his sword to Nauto's throat, and claimed victory.

Nauto stood up, sheathed his weapons, and dusted himself off. He smiled, and shook hands with Astrum, then called the next person to come and face Astrum. Lex was to go next, but declined, after seeing how easily Nauto had been beaten, even with Astrum having no magick. She was still filled with trepidation over Astrum anyway, when it came to battles.

Lamia was then next. She threw off her cloak, revealing tight-fitting black clothing underneath that covered everything but her neck, arms, and her legs up to the knees. She grasped her staff in one hand, holding it upright. Astrum handed his sword, still in its sheath, to Nauto, and asked if he had another staff. Nauto went to his cabin, and brought out a simple brown staff, about the same length as Lamia's staff.

Astrum went on the offensive first this time, and Lamia's eyes went wide. As Astrum brought up his staff above his head, ready to strike her, Lamia squealed, dropped her staff, and cringed. Astrum's right eyebrow went up, and he stopped his strike. He started to laugh, then turned around and started to walk to the center of the deck again, readying for his next fight. Lamia had tricked him, however. She smirked, grabbed her staff from the ground, and swung it at Astrum, who was barely in reach.

Astrum ducked, and heard the passing of her staff above his head. He turned around and blocked her next strike with his own staff, both eyebrows raised this time. He smirked as well, and then twirled his staff clockwise as he tried to hit her again. She raised her staff and blocked his blow, then jabbed at his stomach. He caught the end of her staff with his left hand, and pushed her back. She fell backwards as the force of Astrum's push drove the staff into her stomach, knocking the wind out of her. She gasped, then coughed, and stood up. This time she was really done. She pouted, and then went back to where the group was standing.

The sun had dipped below the ocean as the two fights ended, and now only one person was left to face Astrum: Silen. Nauto took Astrum's staff back to where it came from, and handed him his sword again. Silen walked down, his two daggers drawn, both reversed in his hand. Astrum took out his sword, and held it diagonally, in both hands. Silen smiled, tapped his head with two fingers, and then disappeared without a trace. Vis gasped, as he had never seen Silen do this before, while Astrum simply closed his eyes.

He brought his sword up and over his head, and then slid it down his back, as though he was going to put it in its sheath. It did not go in its sheath, however, and instead made a ringing noise as both of Silen's daggers, crossed over one another, came down on it as he

Meditative Battle

reappeared behind Astrum.

Astrum then swung his sword forward again, breaking the crossed daggers' hold on it, and Silen dropped the dagger he held in his left hand. Astrum turned around to face Silen, and grabbed the falling knife midair, quick as thought. As he grasped it fully, however, Silen smirked, and held out his left hand. The dagger shook in Astrum's hand, flew out of it, and into Silen's outstretched hand.

Lamia gasped, and whispered, "I did not know he could perform magick." Astrum did not know either, but let no surprise show as Silen ran towards him. The way he moved was far more graceful than any elf Astrum had ever seen, and as he ran full pelt towards Astrum, he could not help but to think the question: *How?*

That did not matter at the moment, however, as Silen reached Astrum daggers held high. As Astrum brought up his sword to deflect them, however, Silen disappeared once more. Astrum could deal with his invisibility act, for he did not rely on sight alone. He closed his eyes once more, and heard Silen's whisper of breath, the slight scuff of his shoe as he walked behind Astrum, the smell of his light sweat. He swung his sword till it almost hit Silen in his shadow-walking face, but he did not reappear, nor make any other sound, other than the sound of the movement of air as he backed up quickly to avoid Astrum's slice. *He is experienced,* Astrum thought.

Not as experienced as him, however. When Silen made his way back to attack, Astrum turned around, appearing to be unaware of Silen's presence. Silen noticed this, and walked forward at a slightly quicker pace. When he was close enough, Astrum swung his sword around again, this time letting the flat of his blade make contact with Silen's face. It was not hard, but it still left Silen in a daze, and he reappeared before everyone's eyes. Astrum sheathed his sword, glad all the fights had ceased.

Silen shook his head, then looked up at Astrum and smiled. "Good fight," he remarked.

"Fight?" Astrum questioned. "That was more akin to an assassination attempt." Silen's smile grew wider and he shrugged.

"How can you do that?" Astrum pressed.

"Do what?" Silen innocently asked.

Astrum gave him a stop-fooling-around look, and Silen put up his hands. "Alright, fine, I will tell you," Silen s, still with a hint of glee in his voice. "Let us wait for the others to join us though," the others, not including Ferinus, still at the wheel, were down in an instant, all peppering Silen with questions.

"Hey, whoa, hold on! I can only answer so much at once," Silen protested, and they slowly calmed down.

"I will start from the beginning, but we should go to the crew's quarters to get more comfortable." Everyone agreed, and they made their way down.

Lamia followed the group, her suspicions rising. Was it magick that Silen was using? She did not sense any magickal aura about him, but that could mean that he had a way to hide it from her. Then again, she had never heard of an invisibility spell that lasted for more than a minute, at the most, and Silen had been invisible for far longer than that. She would just have to find out.

They got down to the crew's quarters, and sat down at a round table, which had usually been use by the crew to play games of luck or skill. As they made themselves comfortable, Silen started.

"I am not *entirely* human, I must confess," everyone gaped in awe at him, save for Astrum and Lamia, both who nodded in understanding.

Silen continued. "My father was human, while my mother was a rare type of creature called *senex*. These senex are elven in nature, and live in the same forest as the elves. My father died while I was growing up, and so I grew up with my mother. Her people can blend in with any shadow, and become nearly invisible in the dark. They can also see perfectly in the dark, as good as if it was day."

"For some reason, whether it be because I part-human, or something else, I am not entirely sure, I was far more advanced than any other senex at blending with the shadows and the night." He added as the group looked at him with admiration. "I can become invisible to the eye as long as there is any type of darkness."

The group nodded as one, then Lamia asked, "Well, what about your daggers? How can they come back to you?"

Silen grinned and answered, "These were forged by the senex, and the senex can be great forgers, almost as good as the dwarves. They gave me these daggers to help me when I went out into the world. As long as I supply a certain amount of spiritual energy, the energy that all magick-users have, the enchantments will not run out.

"Although," Silen added, glancing at Lamia "I cannot perform spells, despite having energy of my own. These daggers not only come back to me when I want them to, but can cut through most any material, no matter how hard, as well never chip nor need a whetstone to sharpen them. The only thing they did not seem to cut through was Astrum's sword," everyone looked at Astrum, who shrugged.

"My sword is made of an unidentifiable substance, much like my armor and clothes. All I know is that it never needs to be sharpened, much like Silen's daggers. It can also cut through most materials; in fact, I have never found something it cannot cut through. Oh, and if any spell is cast to harm me, or to bind me in some way, my sword will break its magick; except the curse Umbra cast upon me, apparently." Astrum explained. Silen nodded approvingly.

Lamia had another question for Silen. "Why did you leave your mother to become a thief?" Silen looked at her sadly, and then sighed.

"I am sorry for stealing your gold, I had forgotten until now," he reached into his cloak and pulled out a bag. It was not Lamia's coin purse, however, and she adopted a puzzled expression.

"Whatever I put in this bag will be transported instantly to my mother, for she has a similar bag. I simply have to drop something in, and she will receive it; it goes both ways. I became a thief to provide for my mother's people. They are very poor for all their skills, and I was the only one who would blend in with a crowd in a city. I steal money, and then give it to my people, so they can prosper."

Lamia replied with a meek, "Oh," then she leaned back in her chair.

Silen was definitely not what he appeared to be, and Lamia found herself approving of Silen's thievery, even though he had stolen from her. She saw him in an entirely new light now. Nauto told the group they should get some sleep, and they all agreed, except for Astrum, who made his way to the deck.

Lamia found herself thinking of Silen while she lay in her bed. He was quite heroic, in a way, and Lamia had always admired heroes.

Nauto went upstairs to the deck, and walked over to the wheel. He told Ferinus he would take over, who simply grunted in thanks, and went below decks to get well-deserved rest. Nauto grabbed the wheel, and kept a steady course. He looked down at the door to the lower decks as it opened. Silen walked out, and then, seeing Nauto, walked to him.

"Do you think we could make a slight alteration in our course? All this talking of my mother has gotten me in a mood to see her again," Silen said. Nauto looked at Silen, and then nodded in consent. Silen's face changed from one of anxiety to relief.

"It is only a little bit away from Altus forest, as they live on the border of it," Nauto nodded again and turned the wheel slightly to the left. Silen muttered his thanks, and then made his way below-decks.

Nauto thought of something as Silen reached the steps leading down to the deck, and spoke. "Wait, Silen," Silen stopped and turned around. Nauto continued, "Why is it I have never heard of the senex before? If they are elven in nature, then why is it the elves know nothing of them?"

Silen scoffed, and then answered. 'It is likely you do not know of them because they are not considered "pure" elves. They are considered lowly beings by the elves, and are looked down upon. I do not know anything of your kind, either. But…" He stopped and bit his lip.

"Never mind." He said abruptly, and continued to walk to the door to the crew's quarters, and as the door closed, Nauto sighed.

"I should not have asked," he muttered. He turned his attention back to the water, and guided it smoothly to the elven lands.

Astrum, who was sitting on the railing behind Nauto, turned his eyes back towards the water they left behind. He, too, felt homesick as he peered into the night sky. Astrum did not even know where he belonged though.

Chapter 7

Feigned Wroth

The ship reached the forests by midday the next day. It was more accurately one huge forest, as Astrum saw no break in the tree line, and it stretched on for miles. Ferinus threw the anchor into the ocean, and then lowered the rowboats. Astrum rowed one to shore, while Ferinus rowed the other. Nauto assured everyone that the boats would be safe, and they started their journey into the forest. Ferinus carried a large sack, which held things from the ship that they would need to properly make camp, such as flint, and bowls with which to eat from.

Silen led the group, for he knew the way to the village, while Astrum trailed behind the group. He was sure he felt something akin to the powers of Umbra in this part of the forest, but could not be sure. He loosened his sword in its sheath, just in case.

They walked on for another hour, and Nauto called for them to make camp. Astrum did not disagree, for with every step they took, the feeling of foreboding grew bigger and bigger. Silen, however, did disagree. He argued that the village was only another half hour's walk, and that his mother's people would provide them with shelter. After much deliberation, Nauto finally agreed with Silen, but Astrum could not help the feeling of dread inside of him.

They walked on for the amount of time Silen had told them it would take to get there, when Silen suddenly stopped. He looked up, and Astrum followed his gaze. Above the trees was a thick black plume of smoke.

Astrum looked back down, and saw that Silen had broken into a run, as did the rest of the group. Astrum hurried to keep up, and when he did, he found that they were in a large clearing. Something told him that this had not always been a clearing, however, as he saw the ground was blackened and the smoke that he had seen was coming from the fire that consumed several trees. Ash floated in the air, a grim reminder that a village once stood on these grounds.

He peered ahead as he heard a cry of anguish. Silen was on his knees in from of what appeared to be a burnt-out hut. Silen held his head in his hands, and Astrum heard him sobbing quietly. Nauto was calling out, to see if there were any survivors. Ferinus, Vis, and Lex were busy searching buildings that were still standing. Lamia knelt beside Silen, rubbing his back, consoling him. Silen stood up, and Lamia with him, and he went into the hut, which Astrum assumed was his mother's house.

"Oh, so sad..." something whispered into Astrum's ear.

He tried turning around, but found he could not move, for whomever it was held him in place, and Astrum could not overcome the other's strength. He spoke again, the voice sounding gleeful, though he stood in a decimated village.

"The half-breed's mother died very painfully. Be sure to tell him that, and tell everyone else that you are not to interfere with my plans of domination, Astrum," the voice cautioned, filled with malcontent.

Astrum stiffened even more as he recognized the voice that held so much evil. It was Umbra. Umbra laughed quietly, and let go of him. He threw something at Astrum's feet; it was a bag.

"Tell Silen that this is all that remains of his dear mother," Astrum spun around and drew his sword, all in one smooth motion, but Umbra was nowhere to be seen.

He sheathed his sword, and then looked down at the bag. It appeared to be identical to the one that Silen had showed them last night. Astrum picked it up, and walked over to the hut that Silen and Lamia had walked into. They walked out as soon as Astrum was within ten feet of the door.

Silen looked at Astrum, his eyes red. Astrum said nothing, but instead silently held up the bag that Umbra had given him. Silen gasped, and grabbed it. He reached inside, and grabbed another bag that lay within.

It was Lamia's coin purse. He handed it to her, but she did not grab it, instead, she hugged him fiercely, and it fell to the ground.

She looked up at Astrum, and asked, "Umbra?"

Astrum looked at her, and replied, "Umbra."

Lamia nodded, and then stroked Silen's hair as he grieved for his mother, and the village. The rest of the group converged on them, and they were all shaking their heads, indicating they found nothing useful.

They camped there for the night. They sat around a fire, each very silent. Nauto looked up at the stars. Lex absently poked at the fire with a stick. Vis lay on the ground, already asleep. Lamia was asleep as well, her head resting in Silen's lap. Silen sat staring at the forest. Ferinus sat, observing the tree line, watching for trouble. Astrum had borrowed Lex's bow, and was out hunting.

No one spoke. No one could find the words to say to make it better, for they knew nothing would. Silen's thoughts were sad and enraged at the same time. There was now a true reason for him to fight against Umbra.

A small plume of smoke rose from the campfire as it burned itself out just as the morning sun rose. Lex had woken up an hour ago, for it was her turn to take watch. She looked around at the group as the sun gradually woke them up. Nauto sat up slowly, stretching as he did so. Ferinus snored loudly, once, and the sound woke him up. He looked around in surprise, and then grumbled. Vis rubbed his bleary eyes, and stood up, fixing his sword on his back, which had become askew. Lamia lifted her head up from Silen's lap, and gazed up at him. His eyes were closed, but how he could sleep sitting up like that was a mystery.

Lex stretched herself, as she had not moved since she had gotten up. Astrum came out of the forest, one arm laden with firewood, the other with a brace of rabbits. Lex's bow was strapped across his left shoulder, and across his right shoulder was large buck. As he got to the circle of stones that had once held the fire, he handed the brace of rabbits to Vis, placed the firewood next to Nauto, placed the buck gently beside Ferinus, and handed Lex's bow back to her.

With a heavy sigh, Astrum sat down next to Lex. Nauto started another fire, and placed a small cauldron with water in it on a makeshift stand. Vis prepared the rabbits, of which there were ten. As he finished skinning a rabbit, he handed it to Nauto, who cut it up expertly, and placed it into the cauldron. Once all ten were skinned and cut, Nauto added some herbs and vegetables to the stew, which the group had brought with them from the ship.

After some time had passed, Nauto placed a ladle in the cauldron and poured stew into seven bowls, which also came from the ship. Having no food from the night before, everyone ate ravenously, save for Silen, who ate with far less fervor. As the group finished their servings, another round was served, which emptied the cauldron.

As they finished a second time, they packed up what sparse materials they used to set up camp, and place it all back into the sack which Ferinus carried. They started off into the forest again, this time in a slightly more western direction, though still heading south. Ferinus carried the buck easily over one shoulder, as well as the remaining rabbits.

Lex felt at ease in this forest, as opposed to how she had felt in Senium forest. Her bow was still strung, though she did not have it at the ready. This forest made her feel contented and peaceful. Oddly enough, the deeper they went into the forest, the more she relaxed she felt, although shadows grew long.

After several hours had passed, Nauto stopped, and turned around, a smile on his face. "Welcome the forest of Viridis'nemus, where the great elven city of Nemus Aedes, and my home," he beamed, and gave a flourish. "We will go to my people, to see if they would grant us entry to Altus forest."

The group agreed, and within the hour, they arrived at a small clearing. A large spiral staircase led up into the trees, which were immense, almost unimaginably so. Nauto started to climb, and the others followed. It seemed like forever before they made it to the top, but when they did, they were greeted by two elves. Both garbed in armor, both appearing equally grim. When they saw Nauto, their faces lit up, and they both started to laugh as they excitedly hugged Nauto, who hugged them both back.

"Go right ahead Nauto, as well as the rest of your group," the elf on the right stated, still beaming. Nauto thanked them, and walked on.

What they walked on was a bridge high in the trees. A whole network of interlacing bridges could be seen through the foliage of the trees as the group made their way to the center of the city. The homes of the elves were carved right out of the trunk of each tree. As they reached the end of the bridge, they were standing on a large wooden platform. Elves of many shapes and sizes, though all mostly tall and thin, walked around the platform, which seemed to be a marketplace.

Lex was surprised by the merry nature of the elves. When in human cities, they seemed withdrawn, sullen. Here, among their own people and land they were energetic and joyful. Children played without reprimand from parents, as did some adults. Some young elven men jumped from tree to tree, laughing as they gracefully tried to catch one another. Elven women chatted in the marketplace, heedless of the crowd. This was a beautiful place, free from worry or care.

As they made their way through the throng, the sound of a trumpet could be heard, and the group looked around confusedly, save for Nauto, Ferinus, and Astrum, who looked towards a long, wooden staircase, which led to a large building that rested in the branches of a particularly huge tree.

At the top of the staircase stood one trumpeter, who stepped aside, letting someone else take his place. This someone was dressed like a king, and as he peered down into the stilled crowd, who had stopped at the sound of the trumpet, he spotted Nauto.

He let out a great laugh of joy, and Nauto pushed his way past people in the crowd, and ran up the steps as fast as he could, taking three or more at a time. Once he reached the top step, he knelt down before the man, then stood up and hugged him fiercely. The group followed Nauto up the stairs, and stood behind him as he hugged the man.

As Nauto let go of this man, he turned around to face the group, and said, "This is my father, King Aurum."

The group started as they were introduced to the king of all elves, and they knelt as one.

"Now, now, no need for that, for friends of my son is a friend of mine," the king, Aurum, stated, his voice deep, yet soothing and melodious. He had an ageless quality about him, as all elves do, and his long blond hair fell down from the small crown upon his head. His face was jovial, and as the group stood up, he smiled wider as he looked upon Ferinus. "Ah, Ferinus, welcome back. I see you have stayed with my son for all this time."

Ferinus answered, "Yes, your son is quite the extraordinary elf; I do not think I could leave him even if I wanted."

"I see your speech has improved as well. Fantastic," King Aurum stated. He looked around at the rest of the group, and was about to say something as he looked upon Silen, but then he laid eyes upon Astrum. His eyes bulged, and he struggled to speak as he pointed his index finger at Astrum. This spasm lasted only for a moment, but then he regained his composure.

"You!" he finally shouted, as his eyes went back into his head, and he found the power to speak. "You were banished from ever coming back, why do you return?!"

Astrum opened his mouth and raised his eyebrows.

"But, what, I, uh," Astrum meekly stuttered as he held up his hands in protest, for once lost for words. "I have never been here before, my lord, what have I done?"

As Astrum finally let out that full sentence, it was the king's turn to be surprised again. "Why, you insulted our most beloved Lumen, the woman who is as immortal as you are! How can you not remember such folly?" he seethed.

Astrum again was dumbfounded, but before he could speak again, Nauto intervened. "Father, when did Astrum commit this supposed crime? And who is this 'Lumen'?"

The king looked at Nauto with an expression of astoundment, then of understanding. "Ah, of course. You do not remember for you left before I could tell you of her."

He heaved a great sigh, and began slowly. "Several thousand years ago, Astrum came to our lands, so it is told. He fought off a particularly large dragon, and so a feast was held in his honor. Lumen came to this feast, as she lived in this city then, and when she laid her eyes upon Astrum, she was instantly smitten. He, however, rejected her advances, and so the king, my father, cast him out. I know of his features because there is a mural within the kingdom that depicts Lumen and Astrum together. He matches it perfectly."

Now Nauto looked astonished, and then asked, "Alright, but who is Lumen, and why would he banish Astrum simply for not loving her?"

The king sighed and shook his head. "Lumen is who you may know as the being in Altus forest. She remained there after her heart was broken by Astrum.

Back then, she was like a queen, as she is immortal, but she is not an elf, exactly how Astrum is, as they later found out."

Nauto nodded, and then asked another question, a favor. "Father, we were actually on our way to see Lumen, as we need her help. Would you show us the way to where she is?"

The king deliberated, and grudgingly nodded his head. "Yes. It has been a long time since Astrum has been here, and perhaps Lumen's sadness is not as eternal as she is. But you will not go today. Rest here and we will leave tomorrow at dawn."

He turned around, and walked back into the building, which Lex now saw was a palace. The doors closed behind them as they walked into the hall. The king bid them goodbye, and Nauto followed him as he left. Servants led the rest of the group each to separate rooms, all luxurious.

As Nauto followed his father all the way to the highest point in the castle, which was a high balcony overlooking a vast portion of the southern forest. As they peered over the edge, the king pointed towards a towering tree, which was even taller than the one they were currently in, that stood in the center of their vision.

"That," the king spoke, "is where Lumen now lives. You can make it there without any guide, yes?" Nauto nodded, staring at the tree and the canopy it towered over.

Feigned Wroth

"Good," the king, his father, stated, and he walked away.

He turned around and looked fondly at his son. "It is good to have you back, Nauto," then he made his way back down the stairs.

Nauto stood on the balcony a moment longer, and as he turned to go, he saw another figure coming up the steps that led to the balcony. This figure was feminine, and as she reached the top step, she looked up. Her eyes were large and beautiful, her face much the same, though not large. Her flowing dress sparkled in the failing sunlight, and as she brushed back her blonde hair from her face, Nauto recognized her.

"Dulcis!" he shouted with joy. But as he reached out to hug her, she backed away. "Dulcis, my love, what is wrong? I am overjoyed to see you; will you not let me hold you?"

Dulcis shook her head, her silken hair shimmering. "No, Nauto, you may not," she said, her voice sorrowful, yet still beautiful.

"You left me, Nauto, all that time ago. I can never forgive you. We were in love, but you still left me to go on your 'adventures'," she scoffed; the scorn in her voice did little to diminish its charm. "I pleaded for you not to leave, yet you ignored me!"

The two had always been together. The king had taken her in after her parents, who he was good friends with, passed away from some unknown plague. She and Nauto became fast friends. They first knew that it was love on Nauto's hundredth birthday, which is coming to age for elves. Nauto had been on this very balcony back then, as well, when he wanted to escape from the festivities that his birthday had ignited. Dulcis followed him, and stood next to him. She was eighty at the time, but she was little more than a girl. They had talked, and when they faced each other, laughing at some remark Nauto had spoken, Dulcis leaned in, and they kissed. Thirty years later, and their love seemed unbreakable. Nauto had just defeated the evil wizard, and brought back Ferinus. The elves built him his ship, and he set out the next day. It had been another twenty years, but they both looked the same, for elves do not age as fast as any of the other races. The oldest elf ever was seven-thousand, one-hundred and twenty-two, and he had died just a year after Nauto left. The king, Nauto's father, celebrated his six-thousandth birthday a month before, and it seemed he would live even longer than the aforementioned elf.

This had nothing to do with the present conversation however, and Nauto stopped day-dreaming to look back at Dulcis. She was as lovely as ever, but when he went in to kiss her, she backed away.

"Did you hear nothing I said?" Dulcis said, exasperated.

"Of course I did, how could I not listen to the sweet sound of your voice?" Nauto laughed, adoration filling his voice. "All the time I have been away, I never stopped thinking of you, but it was something I had to do."

"You had to leave me?!" she shouted, "What kind of explanation is that?!"

Nauto placed his hands on her shoulders, and would not let go as she tried to shrug him off. "No, I did not mean I had to leave you. What I meant was that I had to get out into the world, see its wonders, and become wiser. We may have been of age back then, but we had little experience. I needed to leave to become a better person, so that we may live a glorious life. I will continue to travel more, though; I am not quite finished."

She shrugged her shoulders again, and this time Nauto let her go. She huffed, and then walked back down the stairs. Nauto watched her leave, and sighed.

After several minutes, Nauto followed her down, but could not find her. After searching for another hour, he finally gave up. He walked out of the palace, still wearing everything he had walked in with.

He walked to the bridge where the group had climbed up, and, nodding to the guards, climbed down. He reached the bottom, and started to walk under the city. Nauto looked above, and high above the trees he could see the platform that held the marketplace, and could very faintly hear sounds of people saying their "goodnights" to one another, as the sun slowly faded.

The city was as magnificent from below as it was walking through it. The complex interconnection of bridges had always reminded Nauto of a spider's web, though the flowers growing on the tree branches that held the bridges made it seem less morbid than that. It was beautiful, and the forest around him was quiet, letting him enjoy it all the more.

A scream, however, pierced that beauty, and shattered the silence. Nauto's gaze shot forward, and saw some movement past the bushes up ahead. He ran as fast as he could, his elven heritage allowing him to run faster than any man. Once he leapt over the bushes, he landed in a clearing, where he saw an elf being attacked by a forest wyrm.

A wyrm is a small dragon, but with no wings, with only two front legs, and the rest of the body being that of a snake. This particular one was bright green, due to living in the forest, for wyrms had no breath weapons like dragons or dimidium, and instead adapted to the environment they inhabited.

The beast ran as fast as its two legs allowed it towards the elf woman. Nauto started as he saw that the elf was none other than his beloved Dulcis! He became so furious that he did not stop to even draw his sword as he ran towards the wyrm, and instead tackled it head-on. It was a small enough to where Nauto could hold it in one place, but he was not nearly strong enough to hold it when it started to thrash about.

As Nauto was thrown off of the wyrm, it turned its attention from Dulcis to Nauto. He got up, and drew his sword, thinking sensibly once the threat had been taken away from Dulcis. As the wyrm charged Nauto, he glared at it with baleful eyes. Nauto ran towards the wyrm, side-stepped its charge, and swung at its head. His swipe effectively cleaved the head of the wyrm off of its body. Once its head was apart from its body, the creature stopped running, and fell down. It was not yet still however, as its body thrashed on the ground, its final death throes spraying blood around the area. Nauto ran to Dulcis, grabbed her, and took her away from the clearing, away from the writhing body.

The sun disappeared as Nauto ran with Dulcis. Once they reached another clearing, they stopped. Dulcis leaned against a tree, and Nauto fell on the ground, both panting. Nauto looked at Dulcis, smiled, and got up.

"You are alright, yes?" Nauto asked breathlessly.

Dulcis looked up at him, terror fading away from her face. Without a word, she ran to him, and hugged him tightly. "I am so sorry Nauto," she whispered.

Nauto looked at her, and asked, "For what, may I ask?"

She gazed up at him and replied, "I did not mean to be so angry, Nauto." Her eyes glimmered with tears.

"When I heard you had come back, I was overjoyed, until I remembered how you left. After our conversation before, I came down here, to think. By the time I got here, however, I realized I was not mad at you; I just did not want to be left alone again. I did not mean any of the horrid things I said!" she sobbed. She placed her head on his chest, crying softly.

Nauto stroked her hair, soothing her as best he could. She looked up at him once again, and this time, instead of words, she kissed him fiercely. He kissed back with the same amount of passion. They fell over, but still they kissed, their fervor overcoming all other feelings.

Silen sat at the edge of his bed in the castle. He could not sleep, nor did he try. He just sat there, contemplating over many things. He heard a sound, which broke his concentration, and he looked up. Lamia stood at the doorway, a concerned look in her eyes.

"Hello," was all she whispered.

Down in the forest, two worms, the non-dragon sort, crawled along a fallen, rotting tree. They were going in separate directions, both trying to find a hole in the tree for shelter. One of them entered a hole, and stayed there, but the other was not so fortunate. Before it could reach the small, circular crevasse, it was snatched up by a bat, and the bat flew away with its prize.

Chapter 8

Isolation

Nauto awoke. Sunlight streamed through his bedroom window, causing him temporary blindness. After rubbing his eyes, he looked around. His room was exactly as he had left it all that time ago. After the night before, he and Dulcis had made their way back to the kingdom, and they slept.

With the thought of Dulcis, he glanced to his left side. There she lay, still asleep, the epitome of serenity and beauty. A strand of hair lay in front of her face, and Nauto gently brushed it aside. She stirred faintly, but remained sleeping. Nauto crept out of bed as silently as he could, then put on a princely robe, as well it should be, for he was a prince. Nauto then remembered he had never told the group that he was actually royalty, a prince of the elven lands. Almost no one outside of the elves knew of this, as Nauto had not partaken in any of his kingdom's duties. Even his old crew that he had left in Monstrum had no idea. *This morning should be fun*, Nauto thought.

He went down the hall, and downstairs, where the faint aroma of breakfast caught his nose. His stomach growled, and he quickly made his way to the dining commons, where he was met with a small feast. The only ones at the table, however, were his companions; all dressed in clothes much like his own.

He seated himself in between Silen and Astrum. Lex sat across from him, while Ferinus sat next to her. Ferinus wore clothes that the elves had made for him the first time he came to the kingdom, right after Nauto freed him from the sorcerer that held him. Vis sat next to Lex on the opposite side. Lamia sat next to Silen, looking slightly saddened.

She picked at her food absently; evidently she was not hungry. Nauto suspected something more than that, however, but did not dwell on it. He piled food upon his plate, which ranged from exotic fruits to bacon.

He ate eagerly, and halfway through a bite into a mutton leg, he looked up. Everyone was staring at him, save for Lamia, who still looked downtrodden, and Ferinus, who knew who Nauto was. Nauto put the leg down, and swallowed. He wiped his mouth, and raised an eyebrow. "Well?" he asked.

He was hit with a barrage of questions. Everyone wanted to know when he was going to tell them he was a prince, why were you traveling on a ship, how long have you been a prince for?

ISOLATION

The last question, which was blurted out by Lex, was not answered with words, but with an amused raised eyebrow from Nauto. Lex promptly realized that, being the son of the king, he had probably been a prince since he was born. She sat back, embarrassed.

The first question, which was voiced by Vis, Nauto answered with a shrug. "I did not think it was important, as I have not been here for some time. I never intended to take the throne anyway, as my older brother, Ferox, has claimed it; as he should, being first-born."

The second question, asked by Silen, was answered last. Nauto told them of how it was his dream of adventuring, and how the ship was made specifically for him after the sorcerer's defeat. Their questions answered, they were content for the time being.

They each silently finished their food after the brief interlude that had occurred. They each stood up, and made their way to the throne room, with Nauto in the lead.

As Nauto walked through the kingdom's halls, he could not help but to admire their beauty. The wealth inside the castle was neither of gold nor jewels, but of intricate intertwining vines, and the colorful foliage of exotic flowers. Not that the elves had no monetary wealth, simply that they found nature to be more alluring. The companions reached large double doors, and proceeded through them.

The throne room held a vast quantity of plants, and

no two were alike. Many swayed in an invisible breeze, moving of their own accord. One actually looked like a small person, but with the skin of bark, and hair of leaves. It ran around the room, seemingly playing and conversin with other plants.

"A mandragora," Nauto whispered, "It is as sentient as we are, as well as intelligent." The mandragora stopped running, and stood still to look at the companions. It waved at them as they walked by, and they waved back, bemused. It resumed its play.

At the end of the chamber was the throne, which is where the king sat, waiting for the group to reach him. By his side rested a pure white sword. Its hilt and blade were almost indistinguishable as they met with diamond-shaped cross guard, which was also white. It was sharp only on one side, and curved slightly. The pommel held a bright yellow stone that glinted in the sunlight that streamed through the canopy that served as the castle's roof. As the group grew closer, the king picked up the sword in reverence.

"This sword is named Angelus, and it is Lumen's weapon. Give it to her when you greet her, then ask for her help. This is the only advice I can give to you." The king spoke gravely, and handed Astrum the blade.

As Astrum held it, it began to glow a bright yellow, and his sword began to glow a bright green. He turned his head to look at his sword, and then unsheathed it. He held the blades in both hands, and the closer he held them, the brighter they shone. He refrained from touching them together, for he was not sure of what would happen, and looked at the group. They all stared at the swords in amazement. He sheathed his, and shrugged; that would be a question for Lumen.

The group thanked the king, and made their way out of the throne room. As they passed through the doors again, the group stopped as a white cat with a black tail laid in their way. It looked up as they approached it, its green irises glinting with a hidden intelligence.

It walked up to Astrum, who lead the group, and purred as it rubbed against his leg. He gave Lumen's sword to Nauto, and picked up the cat. He stared deep into the cat's pupils, one of which was white as snow, the other black as coal, and then Astrum spoke one word.

"Phasma." Astrum muttered, with a hint of confusion.

The cat stared into his eyes, and blinked once. He placed the cat down, and put his hand to his head. Images swirled in his head in a chaotic pattern. A man cloaked in black slumped beneath him. A woman dressed in pure white crying. A man dressed in blue walking away from him. Two giant beings, a woman and a man, looking at him with curiosity. A being even larger than the two giants combined, sitting on a huge white and black throne, with a grin on his face. A man falling from the sky.

Astrum fell to one knee, groaning. The group surrounded him, peppering him with concerned questions, but their voices were muted and dulled as he continued to witness visions.

The multitude of images slowed to a stop, and settled to one vision. It was himself, flying in the air. He was floating above a large white expanse, nothing around him at all. His eyes were glowing with an emerald glare. He held his sword in one hand, and a magickal jade colored ball of chaotic energy in the other. His sword was unlike it was now; it seemed larger, more curved; deadlier. His cloak swirled about him, making him seem extremely fierce. Four large, unidentifiable wings unfurled from his back. They looked as though hidden behind fog, hazy and indistinguishable. In a moment, however, the Astrum in the vision closed his eyes. He became quite still, his cloak no longer twirling.

When the vision-Astrum opened his eyes, he let go of the glowing sphere, but it stayed floating in the air. With great ferocity he roared (with rage? Joy? It was hard to tell) and sliced the ball vertically.

Everything exploded in chaotic fury. The sound of the explosion intensified as the ground rumbled and shot up and away from him. Fire sprang up into being and swirled away from him. Lightning struck the ground multiple times, and the wind howled viciously. Water rose up from the cracks made from the chaos, forming a giant wave. In the middle of all this, the Astrum in the vision was unaffected, but he curled his lip into a feral smile.

After the explosion, the visions ended. The world around the real Astrum was silent. He then realized he could not hear anyone, for as he looked into the faces of his friends, he could see their lips moving, but no sound coming out. All he heard was a slight ringing. However, with a grand rush, sound came back.

The concerned voices of his companions made their way into his ears, and he raised his hands to allay their fears.

"I am fine." Astrum stated, with no hint of pain or hesitation in his voice. The finality of his voice made the group cease, but they each looked at him dubiously.

They then heard the king from the other room. "Oh, by the way, that cat, Phasma, belongs to Lumen. Take her with you, would you?"

Astrum looked at the cat again, but with trepidation. He picked up the cat, but avoided her eyes. With that, he walked forward, not explaining to the group what had happened.

The Altus forest, unlike the Senium, was absolutely brimming with life. Sound of every kind reached the group's ears. The chattering of monkeys, the low growl of some hidden predator, the songs of birds, a croaking of a frog, the laughter of nymphs running away from satyrs, whose cloven feet made a thumping sound as they hit the ground. Lex looked around in utter awe of the beauty of the wildlife surrounding her.

They had been waiting for several hours now, with the tree Lumen lived in looming over them constantly. Though Lex knew it was large, she could not believe her eyes as it grew in her sight the closer she got to it.

She stared at the group. Silen seemed to be back to his normal self, no longer brooding over Umbra. Lamia appeared sorrowful, however; Lex would have to talk to her later. Nauto held Lumen's sword, while the rest of the group simply looked around them in awe, much like Lex herself. She gazed ahead past the group. They had finally reached the base of the tree.

The tree was absolutely the most massive thing Lex had ever seen. The dragon that Astrum killed near Senium forest was not even half the size of the trunk, and not even close to being as tall as the tree. Lex looked up into the branches, and all she saw was a great green cloud of leaves, totally blotting out the sky. A large spiral staircase wrapped its way around the tree, and went all the way to the topmost portion of the tree. The staircase started right in front of them, beckoning them silently.

Lex looked at the journey she would have to make to the top, and simply stated, "I am not going up there." she would not tire herself out trying to make her way up there. Although she was not too old, she was still not as spry as the rest of the group.

The group looked at her with questioning glances, save for Vis, who nodded his head in agreement. "I hate heights; I will stay down her with Lex."

Nauto shrugged, and said, "Alright, we will not be long." The group followed him up the staircase.

About a half an hour had passed by, and Vis waited patiently at the bottom of the tree. He calculated that they should have reached the top by this time. He looked up at the tree, and was reminded of why he did not want to join them. Ever since he was a child he did not like heights. It all happened many years ago, when…

Vis's thoughts were cut off as he heard a distant shout. The shout continued for a while, and Vis realized that it was coming from above him. He looked up and saw a faint figure falling from the top of the tree! He gasped and sat up quickly. He then saw that it was Astrum!

"--uuuuuuuuUUUUUUGGGGGHHHHHHHHHH!" then Astrum hit the ground with a large *thud*.

Several minutes earlier

Astrum looked up. The tree was somehow familiar to him, though he could not place his finger on what made it so. He now led the group, as the rest of them were basically panting. Being immortal gave him unlimited stamina, for tiring was a mortal trait.

They reached the top, and the group collapsed behind him. He waited for a while to let them recuperate, and then gazed forward. Ahead of him were a small platform, and a doorway to a house that was carved into the tree itself. Intricate patterns were carved all around the door, depicting leaves and branches and animals. He knocked on the door, and waited for a reply.

Several moments passed, but finally the door opened wide, and a woman appeared beyond the entrance. She was quite beautiful, her hair the color of light honey, and her dress pure white. Her eyes were a brilliant yellow, outshining her hair. Phasma, the cat, jumped from Astrum's arms, and made its way inside.

The woman, presumably Lumen, looked at the cat, then back at Astrum. Finally she recognized him, and gasped silently. An expression of pure, unadulterated rage replaced her surprise. She came at Astrum with a fury that would not even have been contained in hell, and she shoved Astrum hard, pushing him back to the edge of the platform.

Astrum teetered for a moment with one foot on the edge, and the group held their breath. Finally, gravity won, and Astrum fell.

"AAAAAAAUUUUUUUUuuuuuuuuuuuuuuu--" Astrum yelled. As he dropped from the top of the tree, the sound of his voice decreased in volume rapidly while he plummeted.

Then...silence.

Chapter 9

Goodly Greed

Lumen opened the door with confusion. She had not had visitors for so long; she could only wonder who it could possibly be. She looked out, and she saw a man holding a cat. The cat jumped from the man's arms and made its way inside. Lumen glanced at the cat, and realized it was Phasma. She looked at the man again, and finally recognized him.

It was Astrum, the immortal man who had rejected her so long ago. She was overcome with such a wrath that she did not stop to think twice as she pushed him over the edge. She peered downward, and saw him falling and finally hitting the ground. She nodded her head in satisfaction, and then jumped off the edge herself. Great, white, feathery wings sprouted forth from her back, and she gracefully touched the ground several moments later.

Astrum still lay upon the ground, but after a while, he groaned and got up. The only thing that saved him was his immortality. Lumen did not sense the aura of magick that usually permeated the air around Astrum, and immediately started to assail him with questions.

"Why are you here? Why do I not sense magick around you? Are you back to scorn me again? Why are you not answering me?" the assault continued, while Astrum simply stood there, dumbfounded; that seemed to a odd reoccurrence in this land. Oddly, like Umbra, her method of speech seemed to be outmoded, and her accent strange.

"What, are you mute, now?" she asked. He shook his head, and finally answered.

"I can talk." his voice small. Lumen regarded him with suspicion. She walked around him, studying him intently.

"Why do you not have a magick aura about you?" she asked.

"Someone named Umbra cast a curse on me preventing me from doing any magick." he answered, his voice returning to its usual confidence.

Upon hearing Umbra's name, she laughed. "Him? He cast this curse upon you? You are the one who originally put it upon him, and now all of a sudden he is stronger than you? Why is he even unsealed?" she scrutinized Astrum with skeptical eyes.

Astrum looked at her, and finally he answered. "I do not remember placing the curse upon Umbra, nor do I remember sealing him. I do not remember you, either."

Lumen looked at Astrum with astonishment. One eyebrow raised, she appraised him again. "Odd," she remarked after careful examination, "You are exactly the same as you were before, but now you do not remember me or Umbra. Do you know of Neque?"

He shook his head. She sniffed in disdain. "Umbra also told me that he was more powerful than me, long ago."

Lumen laughed again. "You must be telling the truth about losing your memory. Umbra was lying, as is his wont. You were more powerful than the three of us combined; Umbra, Neque, and I, that is." She looked him over once more. "Though that seems to have changed. Now, why are you here?"

"Umbra plans to destroy the lives of the people of Solum. He said war is what he wants." Astrum answered. "We need your help in defeating him, as I have lost my magick."

We? Lumen wondered. She looked around. Around them were an elf, a beast, two human women, a dimidium, and a half-breed senex. The elf, one of the women, the beast, and the half-breed all seemed quite tired, while the dimidium and the other woman just appeared astonished.

Looking at the dimidium, she scoffed. "You do know that the dimidium worship Umbra as their god, do you not?" Astrum nodded.

"Yes, but not Vis." he said assuredly.

After several more moments of deliberation, Lumen finally spoke.

"Fine," she replied. "I will return to the elven kingdom and call them to war. I will not, however, do this for you; I do this to stop Umbra." Astrum nodded in appreciation. Nauto walked over, and handed Lumen her sword. She gazed at it lovingly, and stroked the side of the blade.

"Oh, how I have missed you, Angelus." Lumen murmured. She looked towards the group. "Follow me; I have need of some things in my home." She made her way back up the stairs. Nauto, Ferinus, Silen, and Lamia all groaned in dismay, and followed her. Astrum too, followed, while Vis and Lex stayed below once more.

After grabbing all of her necessary gear, she walked back outside. The group silently chatted to one another. "Alright," she stated. "I am done here. Let us make our way to the kingdom."

*War against Umbra...*Lumen pondered. She had not thought such a thing would come to pass once more, at least not for several thousand more years. It seemed that everything was culminating at this point in time however. Umbra's awakening, Astrum's appearance...she briefly wondered about Neque, but shook her head with disdain.

If I win the war and cause Umbra to submit to me, I will be adored by all, not just the elves. She thought greedily. Lumen had been thinking about such a thing within the past several hundred years, but the time had not been right.

Finally, my years of waiting have come to an end, Lumen thought, watching the group make their way back down the stairway. She could not have called the elves to war if not for the eminent threat of Umbra loomed. *I shall wrest this land from the grip of the mortals, and rule over everything. Peace will finally reign over this. No more war, just admiration. Everyone will worship me, and I will have everything.*

Nodding in determination and satisfaction, she followed the group down.

It seemed everyone had gathered in the banquet hall. From Lumen to the king, Nauto's brother Ferox to the entire group of companions and Dulcis, as well as over half of the kingdom. Though many had not met Lumen before, they were enamored with her eternal beauty and gracefulness, both admired traits of elves.

The feast held many delicacies not previously known to the group of adventurers-turned-heroes (save for Nauto, Ferinus, and Astrum, so a little more than half of the companions). Roasted dragon meat, fried phoenix legs, pickled basilisk tongue, and stewed wyvern and wyrm were some of the selections of food that were the *less* outlandish of the bunch.

One of the elves stood up and spontaneously burst into song.

To sup with the elves is a rare event,
During which you have no time to lament.
For gleeful and gay are we of the wood,
And the thoughts you have must always be good.

His voice was graceful and lilting, and it raised the spirits of the room to greater heights. It was an old elvish song only sang at banquets such as this. Other elves soon joined in.

> *From the bottle we drink, our spirits high,*
> *And drunk as a dwarf, till we cannot lie.*
> *The dinner et, 'tis delicious, 'tis grand,*
> *And more will we all of the chef demand.*
>
> *Though deep in the forests do creatures roam,*
> *And elven graves reside in this soft loam,*
> *Tonight we will forget the past and play,*
> *And in the morning strewn about we'll lay.*

Everyone ate and sang with great gusto, save for Lumen. Many elves fawned about her, male and female, all wishing to gaze at Lumen's beauty. Lumen was oblivious to all, however, save for the man who resisted her affections so long ago.

Astrum was currently in a drinking bout with several other elves. He, of course, could never get drunk, and so he drank twice as much as everyone else, laughing at their staggering figures. Lumen supposed it was humorous, but she could not look at Astrum without feeling a blade enter her chest. He was the one she could never forgive.

His folly would not be forgotten.

Chapter 10

Unanswerable Enigmas

Several days afterward

The elves had begun to ready their forces. Envoys had gone to both the human and the gnomish kingdom to enlist in their aid, which Lumen was confident they would have. They had already received word that the armies of the dimidium had been mobilized, and the armies of the centaur and the dwarves are readying for war as well.

The group had received elven armor and weapons to replace their own, except for Astrum, whose armor was better than that of the elves. It was decided that Nauto would become one of the commanders in the army, which was accredited to his royal blood. Lex was also given high ranking within the elven army, although she was human. Ferinus would be a bodyguard for Nauto, while Vis would protect Lex. Lamia and Silen, although neither no real experience in war, were to be given specialized tasks when they arose, such as espionage or removal of spells. Astrum's role was yet to be announced.

Lumen was unsuccessful in lifting Umbra's curse from Astrum, but he was still immortal, and both faster and stronger than any elf in the army, so he was up for any task. Instead, she told him some of the lost parts of his memory; what occurred that time ago, and how it had affected current events, as well as what Astrum would do in this upcoming war.

"Many millennia ago," Lumen started, "four others and I sprang into being. We simply appeared; do not ask how or why, I do not know. At that time, the six main races had reached Solum, and were currently in war with the dragons. We appeared in the vast plains of the centaur and humans. Me, Umbra, Neque, and two others. These other two disappeared shortly afterward, so I do not know their namebs, all I know is that one was a very beautiful woman, and the other was a rather obese, and ugly, man."

"After they disappeared, us three looked at each other with confusion. Around us was absolutely nothing but grass. Three swords lay by our feet; a white blade, and black blade, and a blue blade. I chose the white sword, and named it Angelus, Umbra chose the black blade and named it Diabolus, while Neque chose the light blue sword and named it Medius. It seemed we each chose a blade that was suited for us, as they each glowed faintly as we touched them. After admiring our blades, we finally saw you."

"You lay upon the ground, looking towards the sky. Your eyes were closed, but as we approached you, they opened, and you whirled about and stood up. You had a feral spark in your eyes, that of some primal beast. You stared at us without comprehension, no thought apparent in your face. You grabbed your sword which was next to you on the ground, and charged at us. We raised our swords against you, and we fought."

After a bried pause, she continued. "Just as how I do not know how we came into being, I do not know where we learned to wield swords, or how we knew of anything else, for that matter. We arrived completely sentient and full of wisdom and knowledge. The three of us combined, however, could not overcome your animal ferocity or your skill with the blade. You smote us each down, all at the same time, and then you sprinted off, to who knows where. Being immortal, however, our wounds healed, and we awoke several minutes later."

"We started to talk to each other, and soon Umbra and I quarreled. It does not matter what that argument was of, but it is important that it happened, as we soon decided become mortal enemies; pardon me, *im*mortal enemies. Neque would have no part in it, and went away to somewhere unknown. I gained the elves' love, while Umbra gained the dimidium's fear. We warred against one another, and the dragons, for centuries, in what was to become known as the Race War."

"Before this time, the races had been on Solum for a year, and the dragons had not yet warred against them. Though the legends say of the son of the king of dragons was killed, and the war started because of it, that was not the real reason. I know not the true reason the dragons attacked, but it was after the six races, spurred by Umbra and I, started to war."

"Finally, however, you apparently grew tired of the constant warfare. You had regained your senses, and came to see me. You killed a dragon in my realm, and you charmed me. You then, however, rejected my advances, and I went into solitude." Her voice filled with venom as she spoke, and a sneer appeared upon her face for an instant.

"The elves had no one to command them, and so they retreated. You then went to Umbra, stripped him of his magick, and sealed him inside the forest in dimidium lands. The war between the races stopped, and so soon they were able to overcome the might of the dragons, with your help, of course. No one knows how you were able to negotiate between the sentient dragons and the races, but you did, and then war stopped completely."

"After these events, I heard no more of you, nor did I want to. I assume that it was shortly after the treaty between the races and the dragons that you lost your memory once again."

Lumen place a finger on her chin, lost in thought for a moment. "I also assume that you were here on this world before us three and the other two, and that you had lost your memory back then, as well, for why else would you attack us with no cause?"

She continued with the story. "With Umbra sealed, Neque in places unknown, me living in solitude, and with the treaty, war stopped for a while. There have been many small wars between the races, but nothing catastrophic, nor resulting in massive loss of life."

"With Umbra awake again, war will return to the land, and it will be between all the races. The dragons will return to destroy us, of that I am confident, for this was their land first, and nothing can be done to stop them from joining in with the battles. That is why I must send you out to kill dragons that try to interfere with this Second Race War (which is what I have dubbed it, for it seemed fitting). If possible, find the king dragon, or at least the commander of the dragon armies, and slay him. That will prevent their interference. Also, if you come across any detachment of Umbra's army, dispatch them. You are our most valuable instrument in this war, Astrum. I would go too, but if I take the field then so would Umbra, and that would just mean devastation for both sides."

"Go now, and luck to you." She commanded.

Astrum bid his farewell to the group, and though they had not known each other for a long period of time, he would miss them. He set off on foot westward, towards the mountains of the dwarves and gnomes. The journey would be long, but no real hardships would be had, for what could trouble someone who is as eternal as the world itself?

Silen watched Astrum go, silently walking away from the kingdom. He sighed and turned around. Though Astrum's mission would be much harder than Silen's, still Silen knew that he would have no trouble with it whatsoever.

The moment remained in Silen's head, however, was that of when Astrum whispered something into Silen's ear. He had done so for the entire group, and it was probable that he had something profound to say for each of them.

Astrum had told Silen to not let rage overtake his heart, for then he will become exactly like Umbra, and it is a desolate road he would travel if he did not lay still his heart. He was right. He was among friends, and Silen knew that one day his revenge would come, but there was no need to dwell upon it so. He turned around and looked at Lamia, his eyes bright and clear.

Nauto pondered over Astrum's words to him. Do not let power frighten you, nor let it consume you. Of course, Nauto was now a commander in the army, but the prospect did not frighten him, nor did he feel as though he was any different than before. Astrum must know something that he did not.

Unanswerable Enigmas

Vis laughed silently. Astrum had left him with nothing but a riddle to solve. He asked Vis how a bird could fly if it was too scared to do so. Vis did not know the answer, but he was sure there was a deeper meaning to it than a simple puzzle.

Lamia was puzzled by Astrum once again. He told her one thing, and that was to not give up, and believe. Give up on what, exactly, and what should she believe in? She gazed ahead, at Silen, and was surprised to see him staring back at her, his eyes wide and happy. Now Lamia was even more befuddled.

To Ferinus and Lex, Astrum had said the same thing. He simply told them of how he was sorry. Ferinus believed him to be sorry of the incident on the ship, while Lex believed it to be an apology for the destruction of her battalion at the mountain pass. Was that it however? What else could he be sorry for?

Astrum was uncertain as to where the words he spoke had come from, but he knew deep down they were of consequence to each of them.

But still, he thought as he started to run towards his destination. *What did it all mean, as well as my visions?*

What do I have to do? How am I different? he wondered to himself as he ran. *What does my journey signify? Why does it seem to be a paradigm that I am at a loss?*

Tired of the unanswerable questioned, he strove onwards.

PART II

Chapter 11

WAR

Three months later, the human realm, Arx Fortress

"Archers! Fire!" Nauto bellowed at the top of his lungs.

Several hundred arrows flew by, cleaving the air, as well as the opposing army's armor. The dimidium and centaur were hardy, though, and some whom the arrows had pierced kept running. The elves nocked arrows again, and again Nauto gave the order to fire. Several more dimidium and centaur fell, but the majority of the force kept sprinting.

Nauto looked behind him, and belted, "Draw swords!"

The elves fit their bows over their shoulders so it was wrapped safely around their back and drew their swords. As the enemy grew closer, Nauto drew his rapier and his dagger.

Almost three months of fighting he had endured. Three months of battles, three months of death, but three months of victory. His unit had successfully completed every mission Lumen had ordered him to do. He had secured the western edge of the elven forests along with his brother's battalions, rallied human troops in the east, and fought off every enemy platoon he came across.

Solum had been divided nearly in half; the elves and humans controlled the forests, and part of the plains, while the dimidium, dwarves, and centaur held the desert and volcanoes, the other part of the plains, and the mountains.

The human king had been wary of warring, since they had thirty years ago been in a civil war, and had only just completely recovered, but Lumen traveled to him personally. She had held a small council consisting of herself, the elven king, Ferox (Nauto's older brother) and the human king, King Rector. After much deliberation and persuading, he relented, and lent the elves the human's aid.

The gnomes, however, were not able to be reached by Lumen's messenger, as the dwarves had already captured their king and locked him away, as well as most of their race. None escaped, and the ones that tried were killed.

The battle Nauto was currently in took place on the grasslands of the humans. A small army of centaurs and dimidium held the fortress of Arx, but they committed the folly of meeting Nauto's unit on the battlefield. It

War

would have taken several days to break the fortress, but now that its halls were empty of troops, Nauto could easily capture it. His unit consisted of severl hundred highly trained elves, along with a small human detachment consisting of a hundred or so men and women that had joined them along their way to this stronghold. Ferinus stood beside Nauto, faithfully protecting him, as always.

At that moment, the opposing force clashed with Nauto's own. Nauto slew a dimidium who came within his reach, while Ferinus knocked aside a centaur and a dimidium with one swipe of his huge mace. One of the elves was consumed by a poison mist that a purple dimidium breathed out, and fell to the ground, choking. The rest of the elves fared better, however, as each of their opponents were slain by the swiftness of the elven swords. More enemies came, but it proved to be a small difficulty to overcome them.

The elements seemed to rage across and ravage the battlefield. The breath weapons of the dimidium were far more fearsome than their blades. Fire sprang from a red dimidium's mouth, licking its foes. A jet of water pierced a human's chest, while lightning struck a group of elves.

Nauto passed by a frozen elf, encased in ice by a white dimidium's breath. Acid breathed by an orange dimidium melted the elves and humans, while others became blind once in the darkness issued from a black dimidium's mouth. Nauto encountered a brown dimidium, who opened his mouth and sprayed liquid over Nauto's dagger, which began to rust instantly as it touched it. Nauto dropped his dagger, punched the dimidium, and then finished him off with his sword. From his person, he drew another dagger, and jumped into the fray once more.

The rush of the battle overcame Nauto's senses. All he began to see were those who he had to slay. The landscape became blurred, as well as his fallen enemies. Sound ceased, unless it was the whistling of an enemy's sword streaking towards him.

All he came across met similar fates; death by his blades. He fought very precisely, timing each of his strikes perfectly, aiming for spots that would do the most damage. Those who faced him would find that his agility far surpassed their own, and they could not land a single blow. Nauto had no need to block their attacks; he dodged them all.

Ferinus was the complete opposite. His way of fighting consisted of pure strength. He had to simply swing his weapon and another enemy, sometimes several, would fall. He took many blows himself, though his fur was thick enough to where it would do little damage to him, the spikes on his arms too hard to break.

Together, they formed a duo that was hard to get close to, let alone kill. Nauto pierced at weak point in a centaur's armor. As the centaur began to fall, Nauto jumped onto his back and used him as a spring board. He landed on another centaur and slit his throat with his dagger. Ferinus swung his mace in a wide arc, braining a centaur and a dimidium. Another dimidium struck Ferinus with a sword, but was not able to wound him. Ferinus took the dimidium's head in his hand, and crushed it with brute strength, helmet and all.

WAR

Once the rest of the dimidium and centaur saw how quickly their allies failed, they retreated. Nauto would not let that happen, and yelled "Charge!"

The elves complied and surged forward, roaring along with him, and their grace and agility let them overcome the rest of the troops. The centaur alone made it to the keep, but they did not have time to close its doors. The elves, with the humans lagging slightly behind them, ran straight to the keep, and made it in. Nauto and Ferinus slew the gatekeepers, and urged the elven unit in.

After Nauto's battalion made it in, he closed the doors, with the help of the human troop and Ferinus. There were little in the way of surviving dimidium and centaur in the keep, but those who were alive the elves killed instantly.

Nauto had taken the keep.

Several days later, Nemus Aedes

Lumen looked down upon the giant circular map that was strewn across the table. The elven king and the human king, along with several other commanders, including Lex and Vis, were present at the meeting hall. A messenger burst into the room, panting. Everyone glanced up to look at him.

"Nauto," he gasped, "has taken Arx fortress, milady." Lumen looked up and smiled.

"Good. Thank you, you are dismissed," Lumen stated, and the messenger saluted and left.

Lumen returned her gaze to the map. With Arx taken, the enemy would not be able to gain entry to the human's realm. It was the best possible defensive point they had on that front. She looked from the fortress to the mountains. Is she could take the dwarven city Iugosus, Umbra would not be able to gain hold in any of her lands. The gnomes would then be free to aid in the war effort. From there, she would invade dimidium lands, and so win the war. But first, she had to take Iugosus, which would be no small feat.

Her armies would have to go through the Torva jungles to reach the dwarven realm, and then cross the large canyon of Scindo. Once across, they would be at the base of the mountains. With the city being on the face of Procerus mountain, which was lay in the middle of the rest of the mountains, the journey would take weeks just trying to traverse that treacherous land. Ships would be of no use here, for there were no beaches to make land on, only cliffs.

Lumen sighed, and regarded the group carefully. "We have to take Iugosus. To do that, we must cross through dangerous lands. Tell the army to ready themselves, and to be cautious of the danger that lies in store for them. Lex, you will lead these troops to the mountain Procerus, which is where the city of Iugosus lies."

Lumen looked at the human king, Rector. "Send a large contingent of men to Arx fortress, and a messenger ahead of them. The messenger will tell Nauto and his men to make preparations to leave the fortress and help the army on the dwarven front. He has access to one of the griffins so he may arrive much sooner than on foot. Lex, do not leave until Nauto arrives with his soldiers. Go, now."

The generals nodded, and they left the room, Lex and Vis with them. The two kings glanced at one another, then at Lumen. "You know, Lumen," the Rector started, "You could take the city by yourself, why do you not do so?"

Lumen looked up at him and shook her head. "If I interfere, then Umbra will do the same. I do not want to lose any more men than I have to."

The kings nodded in understanding, and left. Lumen sat down and let out another sigh. War would cost her many followers, but in the end, she will rule over all, and be loved by all, so it would be worth it.

Lumen looked up. "Viator!"

A messenger entered the room. "Yes, milady?" he queried.

"Send for Silen." Lumen answered.

"At once." he bowed and left the room.

Silen walked into the meeting hall. Lumen sat there, waiting for him.

"You called?" he asked.

Lumen nodded, then stood up and pointed toward Iugosus. "This is our next target. Once we capture the city, our chances of victory will vastly increase. I want you to go there, ahead of everyone else, and look for any secret passage in, as well as what the fortifications of the city are. Do not engage the enemy, whatever the cost. With you, we will be able to gain entry and take the city within a week, hopefully."

"All right. Once I do this, when will the army invade?" he asked.

"Immediately after you tell us of what you have found; there can be no hesitation. Oh, and as always, if you find Astrum, tell him to come here to meet with me." Lumen answered. Astrum had not been heard from in three months, and small dragons still plagued both armies. No large ones had come forth, but they were still a nuisance.

Silen nodded, and turned around to leave. Lumen watched him go, but then thought of something.

"Wait!" she commanded. Silen stopped, and looked behind him at her.

"Take Lamia with you; she needs to get out, and if there are any magick fortifications, she will be able to identify them. Do not worry for her, either; I have made sure everything will be fine." Lumen stated, with a slight smile upon her face.

Silen mirrored her grin, though his was far wider. "Thank you, Lumen!" then departed.

Several more days later

Nauto observed the battlefield from on top of the wall of the fortress. Many dimidium and centaur bodies lay across the field of grass. He surveyed his surrounding, and saw nothing out of the ordinary. Nauto returned to the inside of the keep, where his men had set up a dining table, both to eat from and to strategize on. At this moment, it was being used for the latter purpose.

Lamia's map lay across the table. She had given it to Nauto before he had left, a gift, she had said. He gazed upon it with Ferinus and the leader of the human unit.

With Arx fortress taken, the enemy would have a hard time crossing into this realm. It was a good defensive point, but it could not hold many troops, and so the invasion of the land of the centaur would have to wait. *Besides*, Nauto thought, *Lumen would want to take dwarven land first, to secure the best possible defensive positions available. The army would not arrive here for some time.*

He looked up at Ferinus and Veneratio, the human. "Go rest, there is not much we can do as of yet." He insisted.

They nodded, and started to leave. Nauto stood looking at the map for another moment. They had accomplished much in this small amount of time, but for some reason Nauto felt as though the worst was yet to come.

A man burst through the door and reported, "Nauto, you are to pull out your men and travel to Iugosus, the dwarves' kingdom, at once. A contingent of men will take your place." Nauto nodded and sighed. The messenger left, and Nauto looked around the table.

"Tell the men to ready themselves; we will travel as swiftly as possible. We will use the creatures the enemy left here for transportation." Ferinus and Veneratio, who had yet to leave, nodded, and then left.

The creatures, as Nauto had put it, were known as *onus*, usable even by the centaur for travel. They could hold up to a hundred men each, as they grew to be as large as a dragon. They held all the characteristics of a predatory cat, save for the fact that they had large shells on their backs, like that of a tortoise, and they were covered in the scales of a lizard, with the antlers of a buck, making it an abomination.

On each of the beasts there were large, tiered, wooden platforms; it was as if they each held a pyramid on their backs. These made it possible for men to ride it safely. Nauto's men could travel upon these creatures and be at the edge of the elven forests in less than a week, compared to the month it would usually take to travel a quarter of the continent.

Nauto laughed. *Seems to be no end to it*, he thought. He stayed still for a moment longer, and then followed the two.

Chapter 12

Chilling Claws

Silen and Lamia picked their way through the undergrowth of the jungle. It had been an easy beginning, but the path had soon disappeared, and the forest turned to a convoluted mess of plants. The din of the insects became irritating, and the journey proved all together unpleasant. Lamia was quick to agree to accompany Silen, but she now almost regretted that decision. Every so often, Silen would glance back at her, his face filled with sweat, both from the heat of the forest and the exertion of cutting through the growth, but he would smile every time. Lamia did not see any cause to smile at, though.

Finally, though, they reached a small clearing. It was dark in the forest by now, and so Lamia guessed it had to be night. They both collapsed on a fallen trunk, panting. They wiped the sweat off their foreheads, and drank water from skins. After several minutes of sitting there, Lamia felt better. She knew there would be more walking, but they would get there eventually, and it is not as though the journey would be the death of her.

Suddenly, she became aware that the forest had grown deathly silent. The white noise of the insects no longer pervaded the air; their dissonance had ceased entirely. She glanced at Silen, who had also noticed this change in the jungle's demeanor. There was a slight rustling in the trees, as if a strong wind passed through. Silen drew his daggers, and Lamia grasped her staff.

The forest then exploded with movement and sound. Five masked men burst their way through the trees, all shouting war cries. Silen grabbed Lamia's hand, and started to run. He was far fleeter of foot than she, however, and she could not keep up with him. Keeping up with him became decidedly more difficult as she tripped on a root that jutted out of the ground at a peculiarly convenient angle. Convenient, that is, for the masked men.

Two of them grabbed Lamia, and she glanced at Silen. He glanced back at her, this time no smile upon his face. His eyebrows knitted together, and he disappeared into a shadow. The masked men, seeing his disappearance, dropped Lamia in surprise. She scrambled to get away, and succeeded to run for two paces, but they caught her again with ease.

Silen chose that moment to reappear, right in front of Lamia, his daggers at the throats of the two men who held her. The men once again dropped her, but this time in defeat. The other three men held back, for they were unarmed. Lamia stood up, spoke a few choice words of magick, and all five men became bound by vines that shot down from the trees and roots that shot up from below. The men immobile, Silen sheathed his daggers.

Someone started to clap, and a sixth masked man appeared behind the men. He removed his mask, and behind it Lamia could see that he was not a man, but a dark-skinned elf. His skin had a certain purple tint to it, but the most surprising thing was his eyes. They were pure black, and it seemed that his pupils took up the entirety of his eyes. Lamia could not tell who he was looking at, and it chilled her down to the bones. His smile chilled her even more, as it was revealed that his teeth were sharpened to fine points.

Silen snorted in disgust. Lamia stared at him questioningly. "*Alacer*. Dark elves. They are usually used as assassins, for they can see perfectly in the dark, and are as silent as snakes. They also use no weapons, for they are naturally equipped with sharp claws," Silen answered to her look.

This last part was shown to be true, as the bound alacer cut their way out of their bonds, and black claws slipped back into their skin. The unmasked one, presumably the leader, spoke. "Hello there," his voice a biting whisper. "Please excuse my men, for they love to frighten people. My name is Gelu." he mockingly bowed, the fiendish smile still upon his face.

Silen placed his hands back on his daggers, ready to fight. "What do you want with us?" he asked cautiously. Gelu laughed coldly.

"Why, we were sent to aid you on your journey to

Iugosus. The elven king enlisted in our help himself." he answered.

Silen scoffed. "Prove it, or begone from here."

Gelu reached behind his back, and in his hand he presented to them a letter. Silen grabbed it, and read it, his face changing to one of disbelief as saw that Gelu told the truth. He tucked the letter into a hidden inner pocket, and sighed.

"All right, fine. But I warn you; if you so much as touch us, I will kill you without a second thought." Silen threatened, pointing a finger at Gelu. Gelu laughed again, and raised his hands in assurance.

"I am here to cause no harm, of that I assure you." Gelu stated, winking. Silen looked at Gelu suspiciously, but questioned no further.

"Follow us," Gelu said. "You have been traveling for some time, and we have a camp nearby." Silen nodded, and gestured for Gelu to lead them. Gelu then set off into the woods, his men wordlessly following him. Silen sighed, and looked at Lamia. She walked up to him and he put his arm around her. They then followed Gelu into the trees.

The next morning, they left the camp. The night before had consisted of Silen gazing around at the group of alacer, as if they were going to pounce upon him any second. He finally fell asleep, but not before Lamia had told him to calm down. He grudgingly did so, and fell asleep within minutes.

They left the camp, Gelu leading the way, as he

supposedly knew the best path to exit the jungle. Within an hour, they reached the Scindo canyon.

It was absolutely massive. It stretched on for miles in all directions. Silen figured it reached both coasts, as well as the foot of the mountains, which he saw far into the distance, with the canyon ending right below them. Inside the canyon were smaller plateaus, making Scindo canyon a very large maze. Silen heard nothing but the howling wind that blew through the gorge.

Gelu stood at the edge of the canyon. Silen looked around, noticing that the other alacer were gone. Gelu looked at Silen, smirked, and jumped right off the edge of the cliff. Silen and Lamia gasped as one, and raced to the edge of the canyon, only to find that Gelu and the others had simply jumped onto a small ledge that was connected to a natural incline that lead down into the ravine. Silen shook his head, and jumped down after them, helping Lamia down once he landed.

It took several minutes to reach the bottom, and Silen marveled at the size of the canyon. There would be much walking in store. Silen peered upwards as he heard the crack of lightning. Storm clouds were rolling in fast. Silen looked at Gelu.

"We will have to get to shelter, Gelu!" Silen exclaimed over the noise of the wind. Gelu nodded, and started to run towards a large outcropping of rock. Everyone else followed, and just as they reached it, it started to pour with such ferocity that it rivaled that of the storms upon the ocean of Praecingo. The rocks covered the group, though a small trickle of water did come down from in between two rocks in the middle.

Lamia shivered, and Silen held her close. Gelu

looked outside and shook his head. "This does not look like it will let up anytime soon," he said in his customary whisper, though a hint of frustration entered his voice.

"We will have to stay here for some time. Start a fire, Silicis." One of the alacer nodded his head, and produced a flint and tinderbox. Soon, the group had a small fire going. They ate salted pork as the rain fell down. The storm, if anything, had only increased in intensity.

Suddenly, Silen could make out faint sounds of someone shouting. He looked up at Gelu, who had heard much the same. They stood up and peered outside. Nothing was heard but the downpour of rain and the occasional crack of lightning. Then, someone yelled again, followed by a great roar.

Silen and Gelu ran outside towards the noise, Lamia and the other alacer following behind. They rounded the corner of a large plateau, and stopped in surprise at the sight they found in front of them.

A large wyvern was rearing back, its body a muted yellow. Wyverns did not have forelegs and two wings, like dragons, but instead walked on hind legs, with their wings acting as both flight mechanisms and their two front legs. Wyverns were not sentient like dragons, though they were instinctively clever, such as a cat. Wyverns had no control over magick, and have no breath weapon.

Though they have no control over magick, it still permeated the air about them, twisted by their primeval emotions. This kind of magick was wild magick, caused by certain animals when enraged or full of some other extreme emotion. This explained the storm, for yellow dragons breathed lightning, and wyverns would conjure storms when enraged.

What enraged this wyvern was a man who stood in front of it. His hair was a light blond, and cut short. He wore long black pants that covered metal boots and nothing else but plate armor that covered his left shoulder, and his right arm. He held a large sword in his right hand. It was straight and curved outward slightly near the top, but the most peculiar part of the blade was that the hilt was pure white and crooked, while the blade was green. It also glowed with a green light.

Once Silen saw the blade, he immediately recognized who it was.

"Astrum!" he shouted over the wind and the rain. The man glanced back, his eyes widening as his name was called. His mouth widened into a smile as he recognized Silen and Lamia.

The wyvern, however, saw this only as an opportunity. It swiped its tail towards Astrum, white spikes aimed towards him. Astrum turned around, sword ready for the tail. He brought it up and around, effectively slicing a quarter of the tail off. The wyvern roared again, this time in pain instead of rage.

"Attack!" Gelu shouted, and his men rushed forward to do just that. They sprinted to the wyvern at frightening speed, though not as fast as Silen had seen Astrum run. The assassins' claws extended, they jumped upon the wyvern, and tore at its body. They shredded its wings, and pierced one of its eyes. The dragon reared up once more, shaking them off.

Silen ran forward to help, while Lamia muttered a

few words in magick and threw dust into the air in front of her. The falling alacer stopped midair, and Lamia made them land softly on the ground.

Silen took out his daggers, and, still running, threw them underhanded at the wyvern. It had looked down at that point, one of it eye sockets bleeding profusely, washed out by the rain. Both daggers met their mark, piercing the creatures other eye, and widening the gash in the other. The wyvern, still upright, then fell backwards, thrashing.

Astrum ran towards the thrashing body, jumped onto it, and thrusted his blade downward into the wyvern's chest. It thrashed harder, but stilled a moment afterward. Silen held out his hands, and his daggers came back to him. He sheathed them as Astrum pulled his blade from the wyvern, and walked back towards the group.

Silen stared at Astrum as he made his way towards them. His upper-body, no longer hidden behind the black shirt he had always wore, was exposed to all. Astrum had broad chest, though it lean, unlike many whose chests reminded Silen of a barrel. It was defined to the degree that it seemed as though someone had etched the muscle with a fine chisel. His stomach was similar in that respect.

What surprised Silen the most, however, was that his skin was completely flawless. Neither a scar nor scratch marred the surface of Astrum's chest or stomach. Of course this was so, however, as Astrum was immortal, and so he probably could not be harmed.

Astrum still wore a smile upon his face, his teeth like pearls. He held out his hand, and Silen grasped it in greeting. The spark in Astrum's eye was just as Silen had remembered it. Astrum looked behind Silen to peer at Lamia. He waved, and she waved back. Astrum gazed at her intently, and his eyes widened in surprise.

"Ah, you and her, then?" Astrum inquired with a grin. Silen took a small step back, and stammered. Astrum clapped him on the shoulder and laughed. Lamia walked over to them and asked what Astrum was laughing about. He only shook his head in merriment.

Gelu and his men surrounded them, and Astrum looked around, his smile fading.

"These are alacer sent by the elven king to help us with our mission, which is to search for hidden passages into the city of Iugosus, so that our army may invade," Silen stated. Astrum nodded his head in understanding.

"Also, Lumen told me that if I found you, I was to tell you to go to her, for she needs to meet with you as soon as possible." Astrum nodded again, but added a sigh. He looked to the sky, which was beginning to lighten at the passing of the wyvern.

"I will not be going to meet with Lumen," Astrum intoned, his voice dark. Silen raised an eyebrow. "From my journey I have gleaned much, and I will no longer be Lumen's lapdog."

"But why?" Lamia inquired.

"First, let us travel to Iugosus; I will now be accompanying you there. On the way, I will tell you of my new purpose." Astrum answered, though it did not truly answer her question. They started to walk, and Astrum started to relate the story of his journey.

Chapter 13

The Seeker

"When I left the elves three months ago, I had no idea as to where to go. As such, I decided to make my way to the human capital, Moenia, to see if any information could be found. Once I got there, however, I was at a loss, as I was for most of my journey. I did not know what to ask, and I realized how ridiculous it was to ask humans of the dragons, who outlive everyone, just as the elves. Nevertheless, I scoured the city for clues.

"It was there that I found a temple. As I walked inside, the hallowed feel of the building made me feel as though something important was there. No one was there, so I searched the entire building. I walked to the staging area, but found nothing. I was about to leave when I stepped on a plank of wood that made a hollow sound. I bent down, and was able to lift the plank, as well as four others next to it. A spiral staircase led down into the temple's depths. Unhesitatingly, I walked down to investigate.

"What I found was a large library full of musty tomes. I spent a full week poring through the texts that did not turn to dust in my hand, yet found nothing. One book, however, had a picture in it that depicted the war between the races and the dragons.

"The dragons were painted above the ground, diving towards the ground. The elves, gnomes, and humans seemed to be warring against the dimidium, dwarves, and centaur. I figured it must be the First Race War Lumen had spoken of. What I found peculiar, however, were four beings, who outshone the rest in the picture. On the side of the elves was a woman who shone in white brilliance, and, in stark contrast, a man on the dimidium side from which shadows seeped. These two must have been Lumen and Umbra, respectively. More interesting than this was a man dressed in light gray who rode the center dragon. I believe that it was supposed to be Neque, and it was then that I realized he might be the leader of the dragons.

"The focal point of the entire piece, however, was a man in the center of the three colliding armies. He was dressed just as I, and a green light emanated from his being. Obviously it was me, though I do not know why I was in the center of the piece. No description of the artwork was present within the book, but I tore the page from the book and kept it."

Astrum took out the page to show to Lamia and Silen. It was just as he described it. Astrum was at the center, arms raised into the air, with a green glow coming from him. Lumen, who shone a bright yellow, Umbra, who shone a deep red, and Neque, who was a light blue, were converging upon his position, though he did not seem afraid. What Astrum failed to mention was that the sky above Lumen's head was blue, but above Umbra's head it shone a fierce orange. The sun, which sat in at the top of the piece above everything else, was a deep violet. Astrum placed the page back in on of the small pouches he wore around his waist, and continued.

"With one question answered and another raised, I left the city, and walked the vast plains towards the shore of Orbis. The plains of the humans are vast, and it took me several days without stop to reach the ocean.

"I met no one on the way, and so, with the ocean in sight, I began to walk parallel to it. Soon after, I came across a small fishing village. Rumors flew around town that the centaur's were preparing for war. To investigate this claim, I traveled to the tent-city of Tribus Terra, capital of the centaur. It was there that the rumors were confirmed.

"Never before have I seen a greater gather of one race. I have seen the city before, if it can be called that, because it is just a large grouping of tents on the plains, but never filled with thousands of centaur at once. Each centaur bristled with weapons, ready for war. I left the place, for though I am immortal, without my magick I can be captured if a force large enough desires to do so.

"I walked northeast towards the land of the dimidium. It had been a month or so since I had first set out, and I was beginning to doubt my chances of success. I made it past the desert and went to Senium forest, where we had met Umbra. I thought that I could find clues as to what to do or where to go if I examined the stone slab he once rested on.

"What I found was a man dressed in simple gray attire and ashen hair, inspecting the slab. I had a bad feeling about him, and so I drew my sword. As my blade left its sheath, the man looked up, his eyes a bright blue. He had a doleful expression upon his face, and without saying a word, drew his sword against me. It was a plain broadsword, with a bright sapphire in the pommel of the blade, and the blade shining with an azure gleam. I asked who he was, and in a sorrowful voice fit to match his face, he said, 'I do not wish to fight, Astrum, I detest it so.'

"I then queried upon on how he knew my name, though I surmised that it was Neque, another immortal such as myself, Lumen, and Umbra. I guessed correctly, as he told me just that.

"'I am Neque,' he stated, 'how is it you do not remember me, I wonder?'

He sighed. 'Never mind, I do not care, I understand. Do not attack me; I do not want to fight.' I lowered my sword, but did not sheath it; I was still suspicious of him.

"Neque looked at me, and put his sword away. 'You have spoken to Umbra and Lumen, I suppose? The fighting woke me from my slumber on Alio island, and I have come to put an end to the quarrel myself.' I felt relief at his words, for though I supported Lumen's cause, I did not want another war. He had not finished, however.

'Yes,' he continued, 'so I have rallied the dragons once more and intend to destroy all sentient beings on Solum so that the land can go back to what it was before the races defiled it with cities. Nature will reclaim all. That is my goal.'

"I stared in utter disbelief. I knew he was the leader of the dragons, but I did not foresee him planning an attack on the races. I told him that his solution was no better than Lumen's or Umbra's. He shrugged, and looked away.

"'I care not for your opinion. I must go, I am done here.' He had said. Then, much like Umbra and Lumen, he sprouted wings. Unlike Lumen, with her feathered white wings, and Umbra, with his scaled black wings, Neque grew a set of four wings, and they appeared to be just like a dragonfly's wings, but with a tinge of cyan to them. He flew off, wings abuzz, as I stood and watched the ridiculous sight.

"Before I left the forest, I inspected the slab myself to glean information. On it were runes in a language I have never before seen, so instead of trying to learn a new language, I copied the inscription onto a scroll.

"I know not where Alio island is, nor have I heard of it ever before, but it seemed to be his base of operations, and as he was the leader of the dragons, so much as he said, I had to investigate. To do this, I made my way back to the elven forest, via the dwarven mountains, to see if Lumen knew. This is how I ran into you. One more significant event occurred on the way here, however, so gigantic in proportion that it caused me to rethink my position in the war, which I now wish to end for all three sides, including Neque, of course.

"I made my way through mountain passes with ease, as I had in any terrain. Making it around Solum in three months is quite a feat, as it would usually take much longer than that, though I never stopped to rest, only to gain information, and I always took the shortest route possible. On the way through the mountains, however, it started to pour with such intensity that I feared I would slip off the ledge, and therefore have to climb a mountain. To avoid this, I made my way into a small cave I found. I took off my shirt and armor to let it dry, but then I noticed a faint light in the depth of the cave. I put my armor back on, and carried my shirt as I followed the light back to its source to find a young man sitting in front of a fire.

"I walked to him, and sat down next to him. I queried as to what he was doing here, yet he stayed silent. I put my shirt down next to the fire, which I then noticed was black and white, flickering between the two with each pop of the kindle. Without warning, a small flame sprung from the fire onto my shirt, which was consumed instantly, though it was resistant to such things. I gasped, and looked at the man.

"The man wore simple clothing, but had a gray cloth wrapped around his eyes, as though he were blind. He finally spoke, his voice somber, and he inquired of my success in my journey. Deciding to play along, I told him of my success, which is to say, my lack of such a thing. He nodded, as if he expected my answer to be just so, and he removed the blindfold. What lay beneath that cloth I will never forget for the rest of my time, if there be any end. His right eye was milky white, and seemed to stare into my soul. His left eye was just the opposite; it was black as pitch, and seemed to be studying my face. He placed his hands on each side of my head, and gazed deep into my eyes. I became fastened to the spot, literally unable to free myself from whatever sorcery this man possessed.

"After a long time, he blinked, removed his hands from my head, and sighed. He replaced the blind fold, and apologized to me for doing what he did without an explanation. Even with the blindfold it seemed as though he was staring right through me, reading my every move. After several tense moments, he spoke.

"First he told me that he was a soothsayer, and that he had seen my future. He started by telling of immortals in the world are not completely so. Elves are immortal, but only if they are not killed by sword or illness. There are demons residing in dark depths of the world that will live forever, but can be destroyed. Dragons too, are immortal, but only the sentient ones, and are the same as elves. There are different vampires who take souls, suck blood, and steal bodies to prolong lives, but they too, will die eventually by someone or something. In those respects, all of those creatures are mortal.

"The man said six beings exist who are more nearly immortal than all of those together. 'Three of them you already know, Lumen, Neque, and Umbra.'

He told me how all six of these beings were a threat to not just Solum, but to places as far away as the stars themselves. He told me it was my duty to deal with these beings to protect not just this world, but everything in existence. With such an enormous task ahead of me, I asked him how I could accomplish this.

The Seeker

He shook his head, and told me that he could not say, for he did not know. I would have to find out for myself exactly what to do. With that, I only thought of one question to ask; how am I different than the others?

"Before he answered, he asked to see the scroll that I had. I produced it for him, and he read it quickly. Then, in the space below the foreign runes, he wrote the translation in the language of the races. What he wrote looked like this…"

Astrum pulled out the scroll, and on it Lamia and Silen saw the original inscription, which was foreign to them as well, and the translated version below. It read as such:

From one did two new become,
Both different in their way.
Then one left where he was from,
And chaos ensued his day.

The one that was not whole split,
From he did five then exist.
Though powerful he was whit,
Five wrought from him left his midst.

To become whole once again,
He must clear thy opaque mind.
Be free of the world of men,
Be released from shackle's bind.

Merge with the forgotten five,
Then, once more a halve, survive.

"I assumed the scripture had to do with me particularly, for it was on Umbra's slab," Astrum continued, "though this did not answer my question fully, for I did not truly understand the meaning of the writing. I asked again how they were different from me.

"He lifted his head slightly at my inquiry, and did not speak for some time. Finally, he looked at me, blindfold still in place, and intoned words of such enormity that I did not believe him.

"I sat in stunned silence for hours afterward, and by the time I had come to my senses, the soothsayer had gone, along with the fire. I then made my way to the forest, and I ran into the wyvern and you lot. I now realize that I must put an end to Lumen, Umbra, and Neque, along with the other three, though I have not the slightest idea of how to do so, and so I will travel with you, for no other reason then that. Perhaps I will find the answer somehow.

"Ah, yes, about what the soothsayer told me. Though this will surely impede our journey, as you will not believe me and demand to make a stop to talk about it, you should know regardless. What the young fortune-telling man told me was that I…"

Astrum stopped talking abruptly, and looked around them. Silen and Lamia followed his gaze, and noticed that the alacer had disappeared. They quickly saw why, as they spotted an army's worth of dwarven soldiers in the distance.

Chapter 14

Mesmerization

Astrum drew his sword, and looked at Lamia and Silen. Astrum spoke. "We will be captured; I cannot defeat all of them. Silen, flee, I will protect Lamia." Silen's protests were cut off with a raised hand from Astrum.

"It will do us no good if you are captured; you cannot work a dwarven lock from the inside, due to the gnomish machinery protecting it. You must free Lamia and me later. Vanish within the shadows and follow the dwarves once they have us. I will kill as much as I can before that happens." Astrum stated authoritatively.

Lamia and Silen shared a long moment of silence, but eventually Lamia walked to Silen and kissed him on his cheek. "Go," she stated, "I will be fine; Astrum is with me, and he makes sense." Silen nodded regretfully, kissed her back, and started to run away, vanishing as he did so.

"All right, Lamia, stay back; let them capture you only if I am captured, understood?" Lamia nodded, and Astrum turned around and charged the dwarves.

Astrum fought valiantly, taking out many dwarves, but their numbers were too much for him, mostly due to his lack of magick. Astrum was shackled, as well as Lamia, and the dwarves led them to the mountains. Silen bitterly watched them go. He knew that Astrum would protect Lamia, but he still felt useless. He must make up for it by breaking them out of the dungeon.

A new goal in mind, he set out to find a secret passage into the mountain.

Nauto's troops made it back to the forests of the elves, but were having difficulty treading through the swamp they were currently traveling through. They had to leave the onus behind, for the beasts could not travel through such dense woodland, nor tread across the soft loam of the swamp. They were more suited to the plains and the deserts than this terrain. It was no matter, however, as they would reach the elven capital soon, now.

Ferinus trudged behind Nauto, grumbling softly. Every step he took he sunk several inches, due to his great size. Nauto grinned faintly at his complaints. No matter what type of woodlands he was walking through, Nauto always was in great spirits. There was only one exception to that, and that was when he had walked through Senium forest. He shivered just thinking about it, and quickly turned his thoughts to something else.

Nauto's thoughts turned to a small mound of grass in front of him. Like many other small mounds in the swamp it did not stand out, though one feature of this particular mound set off an alarm in Nauto's head. The mound, upon closer inspection, was covered by a plant that was as red as blood, with a pure white flower that had a yellow center. Nauto took out a dagger and cut some of the plants. They shriveled up and died the instant they were cut.

The patch left by the cut plants revealed part of a wooden board. Nauto cut the rest of the plants to find a hidden door. He opened it, and saw steps leading down into the darkness. He told Ferinus to stand and watch guard over the door, as the rest of the troops marched on. Nauto headed down, the darkness engulfing him completely.

Even with his elven sight, Nauto found it hard to see in the pitch black of the hole. Several yards down below, however, Nauto saw a flickering orange light. It turned out to be a torch, which Nauto removed from its sconce. The ground had leveled out, and the corridor turned from dirt to stone. The snapping of the flame was the only sound, as Nauto made sure to make none himself.

Nauto's precaution was well placed. He heard a voice down the corridor that seemed to be chanting.

Nauto set down the torch and drew his rapier, which silently whisked out of its sheath. Nauto rounded another corner and then stood in the doorway leading to a large room. As he peered inside, he saw that the walls were lined with corpses. This underground room was a sepulcher.

The air changed, the room turned freezing. The torches lined against the walls flickered. Nauto's breath turned to ragged gasps. He then realized with dread that the chanting voice had ceased. Nauto walked cautiously inside the room, his hand gripping the rapier clenched tightly, his knuckles white. Something was not right, the catacomb felt unholy, the room filled with malcontent.

As if in answer to Nauto's fears, the same voice that had been chanting spoke. "Yes, you have right proper enough to fear this place," the voice deeply intoned, filling the room with dread. Even Umbra's voice did not compare to the abyssal resonance that echoed throughout the room.

"O woe bequeathed to he who ventures deep, his fate darkened by his certain demise. In the shadows he can only then weep, from the depths he will never again rise."

Nauto stiffened at the words. He gulped, trying to form words, but found himself unable.

"Is it then you, or is it me? You have killed few, while I many," the faceless voice spoke again. "It was a mistake on your part to venture here, elf," the voice remarked. "The roots of the plant travel far, down into this cavern of mine. The bulb, when shriveled, grows a scar; visitors then come to my shrine."

Mesmerization

"Speak, make yourself known to me." the voice intoned. Nauto tried, but could not answer, not while paralyzed by terror of the unknown speaker, the malicious ambiance of the room. Time seemed to slow, and Nauto was caught staring into the darkness in front of him, unable to move or speak.

The torch Nauto had dropped made a crackling sound, and it jolted him back. He was able to speak three words. "W-who are you?" he stuttered. The speaker, a man by the sound of it, laughed, which was an unpleasant and evil sound.

From the darkness in front of Nauto, the only unlit part of the room, a face materialized. Covered by black, shoulder-length hair, the face was pale. Nauto could only see his nose and mouth, the former sharp and curving, the latter a smile, from which Nauto could see two particularly sharp canines which arched down, like a beast.

"Me?" he finally answered. "I am one who feeds, with blood do I fill. Many are my needs, desire to kill." The grin stayed upon his face. He looked up slightly, and the long dark hair parted, revealing his eyes. Nauto gazed in horror at the fire-filled orbs of malice.

"I am Cruor."

Veneratio walked through the swamp, his feet sinking in the mud. He had followed Nauto to fight with him in Iugosus. Nauto was a valiant elf, and Veneratio looked up to him in great admiration. Nauto's stratagems succeeded with alarming regularity, and they were masterpieces of great care and craftsmanship. He wanted to go over the plan, but could not find him among the troops.

Veneratio peered ahead, and spotted Ferinus standing by a mound of grass. As he got closer, Veneratio saw that the mound hid a passageway underground. He glanced up at Ferinus.

"Is Nauto down there?" he inquired. Ferinus grunted in answer, nodding.

Veneratio nodded, and went down the passage. It was pitch black, so he had to feel his way around by keeping his hand upon the damp wall of dirt, which quickly changed to stone. Deep in his gut, he had a bad feeling of this place, and he drew his bow and nocked an arrow, keeping his back to the wall to guide him.

Up ahead, he saw a flickering light. A dropped torch on the ground, and a figure standing by it. He could tell by the hair that it was Nauto, but why was he standing still? Veneratio kept his arrow nocked and crept up behind Nauto to see what was wrong. He peered over Nauto's shoulder.

Nauto felt a whisper of breath behind him, and the light touch of it shook him from his fear. He turned around to see Veneratio standing behind him, bow at the ready. The word 'run' came to Nauto's lips, but did not escape them. Veneratio saw Cruor, and was immediately gripped by the same fear that had Nauto in its grip. With great effort, however, he was able to lift his bow and release the arrow, which flew into the darkness and clattered to the floor.

Nauto gritted his teeth as Cruor laughed again. He dare not turn around to gaze into the shadows, for he knew he would be petrified if he did. Something about Cruor's visage had an effect on him, and not just him, as Veneratio was as still as he had been.

"What do you want?!" Nauto shouted in desperation.

Nauto felt a presence just behind him. "What I want?" Cruor whispered from Nauto's shoulder, his breath acrid and cold. "I do not want; I need. I need to hunt; then feed."

Nauto felt a chill run up his back, and again he was unable to move; it seemed the man's very presence could hold him fast in place, petrified. It was both a magickal and purely instinctual fear, it seemed.

The man spoke again. "What, though, pray tell, are you two doing in this bog? No one has come here in such a long time; I thought I might have outlived everyone."

The paralysis loosened slightly, and Nauto was able to answer. "W-we were p-passing through to reach the r-r-realm of the dwarves. We go t-to war." Nauto quaked.

"Ah, so it has happened again? It has been some time since the last. Who is fighting, and who leads them?" Cruor asked, his hand lightly gripping Nauto's shoulder. Nauto could see that Cruor's fingernails were black as jet, and filed to points.

Nauto cleared his throat. "The elves, humans, and gnomes f-fight against the dimidium, centaur, and d-dwarves. It is an immortal named Lumen who leads the former three, and another named U-Umbra leads the latter three."

Cruor hissed in distaste. The paralysis fled Nauto's body, as well as Veneratio's. They quickly moved away from Cruor, whose face was filled with great wrath. His hands gripped his head, and his eyes bulged. The manic fit soon passed, however, and Cruor stood up straight. His eyes had cooled, turning to an icy-blue color.

Cruor's voice had no trace of the evil that it contained before as he spoke, though the anger remained. "Umbra," he seethed, "He paid me grand insult and injury, once. You two go to war against him? That is folly." Cruor suddenly burst into a fit of maniacal laughter, completely a different person than he was just a moment ago.

Nauto, wary of Cruor still, grasped his rapier tightly. "Lumen has the power to match him, as well as another being, who is also eternal, called Astrum." Cruor stopped laughing, and raised an eyebrow. He placed his hand on his chin, musing over the names.

Nauto glanced at Veneratio, who still slightly trembled. He looked back to Cruor, who was lost in thought. Nauto dared not leave, for he dreaded the thought of Cruor doing horrible things to the both of them. Never before had he been so frightened of a man. Though this was no ordinary man.

What is he, a sorcerer? A demon? Nauto thought. Whatever the case may be, he must leave this place, and get away from Cruor.

That was not to be, however, as Cruor looked at Nauto and Veneratio, his eyes filled red as flame once again. "I will fight with you, against Umbra. You will find me a great ally in this war." Cruor said, licking his lips. "I lust for his demise."

Nauto and Veneratio glanced at each other, unsure. Cruor allayed their fears, however. "I promise I shall not harm you or your comrades." he remarked with a flourish. Nauto was about to say no to his proposal, but his terror of Cruor stopped him from doing so.

Even if Nauto stated otherwise, Cruor would not have had it. He looked up and met Nauto's eyes. "Besides," he smiled, "I will *not* let you refuse my offer. Be it your death or your enemies, my hunger will not be sated until Umbra is gone."

Nauto, grudgingly, nodded his head. Cruor smiled, his sharp canines glinting cruelly.

Chapter 15

Slim Success

Lamia fell to the ground in a cloud of dust. The hard stone floor was cold and unforgiving. Astrum was thrown next to her, though he was able to land more gracefully. The cell doors shut with an iron clang. For short beings such as dwarves, they sure were strong.

Lamia studied the cell. Its only occupants were Astrum and herself. The dwarves had confiscated their weapons, as well as Lamia's spell components, and nothing could be done. She turned to Astrum, who looked at her and simply smiled crookedly.

Confident as ever, he said, "Silen will come, I am sure of it; do not worry." He then proceeded to lie down and close his eyes, apparently trying to sleep. How could Astrum be so carefree? As an immortal, a certain degree of assuredness would be expected, but only for his own wellbeing, not for others. It was not like he was arrogant either, he simply believed in the man he knew for a short amount of time.

How was Silen supposed to infiltrate the kingdom all on his own, regardless of the usefulness of his skills on the matter? Just like Lumen, Umbra was bound to have a few magick-users at his command, regardless of their small numbers and their illegal practices. They could readily find Silen even if he was blending with the shadows. Lamia had not lost all hope, though she found his chances slim, at the best. Absently she sat down and rested a hand on her stomach, rubbing it gently.

Silen had followed the dwarven troops for some time, but as they entered the mountain through a huge metal gate, he stopped to ponder how to get inside. He needed to find a secret passage to give access to Lumen's troops and to free Lamia and Astrum, as well as...no, he must not think on it, but instead he put all his energy into searching the craggy wall of the mountain.

It was now dark outside, so Silen could cloak himself and walk to the right of the main gate. He walked for several minutes, but the unforgiving wall of the mountain seemed to hold no seams of secret doors, nor any small caverns with which to enter. Exasperated, he turned around and headed the opposite direction. He passed the main gate again, but just as the right side, the rock had no flaws that would suggest a hidden passage.

Usually, Silen could tell the difference between a wall and a secret door, as many noble houses held hidden rooms accessed by certain mechanisms; a discoloration of the wall, the change of the air flow or temperature in a certain passageway, or even, and more conspicuous, a small keyhole in the middle of a blank wall. None of these seemed to present on the mountain side, though Silen hardly thought it would be as blatant as a keyhole.

A small sound could be heard behind him. Still cloaked in shadow, Silen whirled around silently, a hand on the pommel of one of his knives. It had sounded as if someone had spoken, though no one was there to be seen. Cautiously, Silen stalked his way to where he had heard the sound, knife ready to be drawn.

A head poked out at a downward angle from the mountain in front of Silen. Silen's expression changed from one of suspicion to incredulity, his mouth opening wide. A hand came out along with the miniature head, and it made a signal to be quiet.

Silen closed his mouth.

"Follow me." the head whispered.

Silen dumbly nodded, and went over to the head. It disappeared, and soon a hidden door opened wide, and Silen quickly made his way in. The door shut behind him, and he was left in darkness.

"Put on these," a voice spoke from behind Silen. "Help you see." Silen turned around and saw a glint in the dark. He blindly grasped them.

It was some form of ocular device, and as he put them on, the room became bathed in a green light. He took the device off, only to find that the room had not gotten brighter, but the eyewear made the room seem full of light. Bemused, Silen put them back on.

"Good. Follow me." the voice commanded, this time from below Silen. He looked down to see a small being, presumably a gnome, going down a corridor. Silen followed the gnome into the mountain, too amused by the situation to be cautious.

Several minutes of walking passed by, and suddenly Silen found himself in a large cavern. Several other gnomes milled about, exchanging sparse words with each other as they passed by.

"Direction room," the gnome leading Silen explained, "Go down passages. Reach different places."

Silen did not know if the gnome talked to Silen as if he was a child, or it was how gnomes regularly talked. Regardless, Silen peered about the room to find that many different passages lay before him, all heading in separate directions.

Silen peered downward at the gnome, and asked, "What is your name?"

The gnome regarded Silen, the device large on his head, took a deep breath, and stated with grandeur, "Navitasapparatussupellex. Call me Navi. Come now." Navi grabbed Silen's hand, and led him down one of the many passages going into the mountain.

Just how many turns Navi took Silen down he did not know; the labyrinth was veritable indeed. Though Silen's duty was to find a secret passage into Iugosus, this route seemed far too complicated and narrow for an entire army to travel through.

Navi stopped suddenly after about an hour of walking, and Silen realized that the winding corridors of stone had stopped, and another cavern took their place. This wide space held many more gnomes than the other, and machines of some sort lined the walls. Gnomes, all with goggles on, tinkered with the machines. One machine was attached to a gnome's arms, and another to his legs. The gnome, with these machines, leapt around the room and lifted heavier parts for other gnomes to work on their respective machines. It was all very confusing to Silen's eyes, as apparent on his face.

Navi looked up at Silen, and led him to the far side of the cave. A wizened gnome was talking with two others, apparently giving them advice on their blueprints, which one held in his hands. The two gnomes walked away, and the older gnome peered at Navi and Silen. His goggles whirred with power, the right side extending outward, while the left widened.

Finally, after much scrutiny, the gnome held out his hand for Silen to shake. Silen did so, and asked, "What is this place?"

The elder gnome coughed, and then answered, "The mountain we are in holds one of the lesser dwarven cities. We gnomes have built secret passageways to use in each of the dwarves cities for our own purpose. This is the machinery room. Here we gnomes work on developing new technology. This particular room, however, is temporary, as the dwarves have enslaved many of our kind and do not allow us our usual work space. I am the king of the gnomes."

He took a deep breath, just as Navi had, and Silen feared another long name. "Indoles. Who are you?"

"My name is Silen. I come from the elven lands to

scout the dwarven city in preparation for battle." Silen then added, "I thought the king had been captured."

Indoles chuckled, and replied, "We replaced me with a mechanical gnome replica. It fooled the dwarves for awhile, long enough for me to escape their clutches. The cell they had placed me in is actually just on the other side of this wall." He pointed behind him to a blank rock wall.

A gnome came up and spoke to Indoles, "Throwing machine complete. Test it?"

Indoles nodded, and Silen asked another question as the gnome walked away. "Why do you speak so eloquently, yet the other gnomes talk fragmented?"

Indoles then explained. "The king of the gnomes is chosen because he is the most intelligent and knowledgeable of all other gnomes. To keep up this image, I speak as such. It is not that other gnomes cannot speak fluently, they prefer not to, as mincing words is not a pastime of ours. I also speak like this because of relations to the other races, for diplomacy."

Silen nodded, though the expression on his face suggested that he still did not quite understand, so he changed the subject. "Why have you not contacted the other races; the elves and the humans?"

They were interrupted by a small gnome who flew through the air, screaming, arms flailing. He flew past the king and Silen, and landed in a net several yards away. He sat up, dazed, and looked at the king. "Needs work." he muttered, then slumped down.

Indoles coughed nervously, furrowed his brow, and finally responded, "We gnomes fight for ourselves; we did not want the other races thinking we were weak, so we devised a plan to conquer the mountain without their help."

Silen nodded. "You know, an elven army is on its way to liberate you," Indoles looked up in surprise. "Do you still want their help?"

Indoles shook his head furiously. "No! Call them off! They will not gain entry here without our help, and we do not plan to give it."

"It was my duty to find a secret passageway to ensure that help could arrive safely, how can I abandon my orders?" Silen asked with a slight smile.

"You not needed. Leave now!" Indoles shouted, his formerly fluent speech broken.

Indoles took a deep breath, and calmed down considerably. He mused upon what he should do, and finally came with an answer.

"The army is on its way? Then they will come to see us fight in all our glory. The battle will take place inside the city of Iugosus, which is carved into the mountain next to this one." Silen's eyes widened with surprise, and Indoles explained. "You have traveled a long way from the great gates that guard the pass to the city."

The gnomish king cleared his throat and continued. "The halls inside the castle at the top of the city are spacious. The dwarven army trains there, as well. We will take them by surprise, as the plan I devised is monumental! The elves will see it come to fruition." He rubbed his hands together gleefully.

Silen nodded, though he could not possibly see what the gnomes could do that would impress the elves. The king started to walk away, but Silen tapped him on the shoulder. "Eh? What do you need now?" Indoles asked.

"There is still one more thing I need." Silen said with a small wink.

Lamia had fallen asleep, just like Astrum. The ground was harsh to sleep on, but exhaustion had taken over. She had not slept well for some time, so the hard floor was more than enough to satisfy her, for now.

Lamia awoke, however, as she heard a small but repetitive noise. She blearily looked around the room. Astrum had already awoken, and had placed his ear against the back wall of the cave. Lamia joined him, and gazed at him questioningly. He simply shrugged.

The tapping got louder, as well as a sound coming from outside the cell. Astrum and Lamia left the wall to peer out of their cell. Down the hallway sounds of a fight could be heard. Suddenly, however, the tapping and the commotion outside ceased, and all grew silent.

The events happened simultaneously. Hooded figures burst down the stairs and into their cell hallway, and the wall behind Lamia blew up, and a billowing black smoke pervaded the cell. Coughing, Lamia looked around in awe. Six figures had barged into the cell. Behind Lamia, a man blackened with dust walked into the cell from the former wall.

Completely synchronized, one of the hooded men and the dust-covered man said, "We have come to save you."

Lamia realized then that the hooded men must be Gelu and his men, and the blackened man must then be…

"Silen!" Lamia cried with delight as she threw her arms around him. Astrum, less excited than she, nodded to Gelu, who seemed slightly peeved. Gelu unlocked the cell with one of the guard's keys, and walked inside. A small troop of tiny men, presumably gnomes, then walked into the cell from the hole in the wall. They shook each other's hands in delight, and many high-fives were given.

Lamia released Silen, and looked at him inquiringly. Silen wore strange goggles, and had a gnome clinging to his shoulders. He shrugged, which was quite difficult with his passenger, and whispered, "Tell you later."

Then, raising his voice, he said, "Follow me." He gestured into the hole, and walked inside. The others followed him into the dark passageway.

Nauto glanced warily at Cruor. Before leaving, Cruor had collected his things, though this consisted only of a monstrous, jet black, two-handed sword and a voluminous black cloak. The cloak shrouded his entire body, and he wore it though the marsh air was oppressive. He held the sword with ease in one hand, as though it was weightless. The way he held it made it seem as though it was an overturned cross. Nauto began to feel like bringing him along was a bad idea.

They caught up to the rest of the regiment, and the elves too treated Cruor with caution, often making way for him when he proceeded to close to them. An older elf approached Nauto and whispered into his ear. Nauto's expression changed from one of suspicion to grim as the elf continued to talk. When he was done, he walked away, looking meaningfully at Cruor.

Nauto sighed and approached Ferinus. "Keep an eye on Cruor," he whispered. "Make sure he does not make any odd movements." Ferinus nodded and moved closer to Cruor, needing no explanation.

Veneratio glanced at Ferinus, then at Nauto. "What is wrong?" he asked Nauto, who gazed at him silently.

"It appears," Nauto heavily sighed, "That our new 'companion' is what is known as a vampire, a demon of sorts."

Veneratio stared dubiously at Cruor, then at Nauto, who continued. "He feeds on blood to survive, and is apparently immortal. He has increased strength, agility, and so on, making him *superior* to mortals, although, as that soldier told me, a vampire's passion is also increased, making him doubly dangerous, as if he was not already so. Most likely he is also insane. I do not know of what happened between Cruor and Umbra, but let us be thankful he is on our side, for now, at least."

Veneratio clasped his sword tighter, his knuckles becoming white. A monster such as this within Lumen's ranks? He could not see this temporary alliance ending well.

Silen stared at the king's plans in disbelief. Such a thing did not seem quite possible in any sense of the word imaginable. The king himself seemed very proud and confident in it, however, and so Silen did not raise a dispute. Lamia, too, stared at the plans with an expression akin to first laying eyes upon a cat with several heads and extra tails.

"How can such a thing be possible?" Lamia marveled, her voice slightly quivering.

Indoles crossed his arms and smirked. "The dwarven king, Adamans, cares for his people greatly. He, expecting his city to be attacked, has evacuated all citizens, leaving only himself and his army." the gnomish king said, still smiling. "The outside of the city, which is carved into the mountain, has been emptied. The king sits on his throne inside the mountain, and, as I have mentioned before, the army trains in those halls as well. This means everyone who would be a part of this battle is behind the city, so to speak, within the mountain. That is why this plan cannot fail, for they will not even know we are coming."

"What manner of sorcery can achieve this goal" Lamia asked in amazement.

The king beamed. "Absolutely none. It is pure engineering done by us gnomes."

Silen crossed his arms, mulling over the situation. *With this, the war could turn directly into our favor*, he thought.

Gelu smirked, delighted in the fact that the dwarves would be taken by complete surprise by the gnomes. Astrum smiled as well, as the war would be over sooner than he had first thought, if all went well.

"Would you like to see the machine?" Indoles asked, his voice filled with merriment. Lamia excitedly nodded, and followed the king as he walked off, the rest close behind.

Chapter 16

On The Move

Nauto had reached the elven kingdom, along with his troops. He spoke with Lumen, and she had told him of Silen and Lamia. Eager for the companions to come together again, he searched for Lex and Vis. After a joyful reunion, they set off. The number of soldiers rose to approximately two thousand now that their forces had combined into one. It would be a long journey with such numbers, but they would surely take the city.

Seeing the design come to life was truly breathtaking, especially one that seemed so ludicrous.

Lamia, Silen, and Gelu all inspected the machine closer, while Astrum stood next to Indoles.

"There are two more in separate rooms. With these, we will overtake the city effortlessly." the king stated with a glint in his eye. "We will come from the west, and since the city faces to the east, the elven and human forces will see the usefulness of the gnomes in action. That is when we will commence, at dawn, when the army is in the plains below Iugosus. We will first attack the gate of the dwarves that leads to their city, and leave them wide open. When the army arrives in the plains below the city, we will strike."

Astrum glanced at the king, whose gleeful fervor was contagious. "I will dispatch the dwarves at the gate for you." Astrum remarked boldly.

The king laughed at the absurdity of this declaration, not knowing Astrum was capable of such things. His smile wide, Astrum walked off towards the outside of the caves. Indoles watched him go, his smile fading as he realized Astrum was serious.

"Wait!" he shouted, and took off after Astrum. Silen, Lamia, and Gelu looked up from their inspection, glanced at each other, and then followed the panicking king.

Two weeks later, Scindo canyon

Unlike when Nauto had returned from the Arx fortress, it took him and his army, along with the soldiers under Lex and Vis, twice as long to travel a quarter of the continent. Still, how they had achieved such distance in half the time it usually took was miraculous, though they did not have the aid of the onus. This may have been due to the high morale of the troops. They traveled, burdened with equipment, with almost no rest, for the entirety of the trip. Not once was a complaint raised, and Nauto was proud of his men. This was the true worth of the races when working together.

Nauto glanced back at his soldiers, and spotted Cruor. He was walking with the rest, but the others kept a noticeable distance away from him. His face was frozen in a fierce grin, apparently excited by the prospect of war, or, more likely, blood. During the day he had to be covered in multiple blankets to protect him from the sun. Nauto would have his men give them theirs during this time, but the problem was that they did not want them back afterwards. In this fashion they had traveled.

The army climbed out of the canyon, and the gates leading into the mountains could be seen in the distance.

The grandeur of the gates could immediately be recognized, as they appeared colossal even from so far away. It would take two hours or more just to reach it, even more so if Nauto's prediction was proven to be true, which was that the dwarves would start their resistance before they could reach the city.

The gnomish king shook his head, still baffled from

the events that occurred a fortnight ago, or, rather, the *lack* of events. Astrum had traveled to the gates to take the dwarves by surprise, yet there was none there. It seemed that the entire area had been deserted by the dwarves. Indoles had ordered then ordered some gnomes to spy on the city of Pupillus, which is where Lamia and Astrum had been held prisoner, but the spies reported back that no dwarves were there, either. The entire force of elves and men could pass through unmolested, but with no assistance by the gnomes.

Indoles sighed and massaged his temples. Although he had told Silen and the others that his inventions would win over Iugosus, they had never actually been tested. Mathematically, everything should work as intended, but there could still be a mistake made somewhere that would cost them everything. One of the machines would be more than enough to take over the city, but he had made three as a precaution.

A gnome walked into the king's temporary throne room. "Army is at gates. Proceed?"

Wearily, the king nodded his head, and stood up. He followed the gnome out to the deployment area, which was behind the mountain, on the opposite side of where the city was. He was not quite ready to unleash his machines, but they had to be used now or never if he was to prove the gnomes' worth to the other races. The mission would cause no blood to be shed, from either side. It was the pure genius of the king, in fact, and he had to invent the new machines simply to execute it.

"We launch at dawn." he announced to the gnomes, as well as Lamia and Silen. "Hopefully the immortal can keep the elves from storming the city until then.

Nauto was very confused. No force of dwarves came out to meet them, nor was any guarding the gates. It was night by the time they had reached the mountain side gates, but no one, dwarf or otherwise, was there to defend the monstrous metal doors.

Puzzled, he peered upwards at the top of the gates, where there was a narrow pathway one could walk across, built into the gates. He could see a small figure there, but it was so far he could not tell who or what it was. It appeared to be that the figure was waving, but Nauto could not be sure.

Nauto then realized the figure was growing bigger and bigger, as though he was turning from a bug to a man. This was not the case however, as Nauto's bewilderment turned to horror as he realized the person was falling towards the ground at an alarming speed. He backed up quickly, as did the troops behind him who had also witnessed the descent of the figure.

It seemed to be an eternity before the figure hit the ground with a resounding crash. The ground cracked slightly with the force at which the person was falling. Nauto gasped when the figure finally hit the ground, though he knew it was going to happen. Lex, who was standing next to him, yelped.

For several moments, everyone was still, save, that is, the person who hit the ground. For someone who had fallen so far, he was doing surprisingly well, enough so to stand up and dust himself off. Nauto continued to stare, not comprehending the nature of the man. When the man looked up, however, all the tension left Nauto's body in a breath he had not realized he was holding.

The man was Astrum. Though Nauto could have thought of a few better ways to greet his friends that did not involve in dropping several hundred meters to the ground, he was glad all the same that it was Astrum who had done so, as he was the only one who would have survived such a thing.

The elves and men behind Nauto raised their weapons to fend off the supposed attacker, but Nauto calmed them with a wave of his hand. He walked up to Astrum, arms wide, and gave him a warm, welcoming hug. Ferinus and Vis did much the same, but Lex opted to slap Astrum instead.

"You scared me half to death!" she protested angrily. Astrum could only laugh heartily at her rage, which made her even more upset. Soon however, the five of them were all laughing, with all the troops behind them glancing at each other, utterly perplexed.

The gates started to open, and a deafening grating sound came from them. The troops covered their ears in pain. Soon the noise stopped, and they breathed a sigh of relief. The gates only opened slightly, though the gap it created was more than enough for the army to pass through together.

Nauto walked apace with Astrum. He had so many questions, but did not know what to ask first. Astrum glanced at him out of the corner of his eye and grinned. "Just wait; you will find out." he said. Nauto did not want to wait, but it seemed he had no choice but to do so.

They walked through the darkened pass, cliffs on both sides. Nauto looked upwards, fearing an attack from above, but Astrum assuaged his fears with a simple, "Do not worry."

As if he could simply do that. They were in the middle of the enemy's territory, and only had the words of an immortal with no sense of caution to reassure him. Nauto kept tense, wary of an ambush. The passage started to curve towards the east, meaning they were getting closer to the sea of Orbis. That would make sense, as the dwarven/gnomish capital was said to face Orbis Sea. After some time, the passage started to straighten out, then go back towards the west, meaning the end of the rift would face them towards Iugosus.

The rift between the two cliffs widened, and the mountain lay a long distance ahead of the army. Nauto could see the dwarven city, sitting on the side of the mountain.

The army had marched to the halfway point in between the gates and the city when Nauto ordered them to stop. The plains they walked upon were totally unlike those in the human realm. The landscape was sparse and largely barren; instead of grass there was only stone, with small shrubs dotting the area.

The higher the city was up the mountain, the more orderly it seemed to be. It started at the base of the mountain as a sprawling urban area, each stone house placed haphazardly next to the other. The organization of the buildings gradually increased as you traveled through the marketplace, then up to the nobles' area, then finally to the kingdom itself, whose towers rose above the peak of the mountain. Each building was in the form of a cube, the most expensive houses consisting of dozens of such cubes.

The entirety of the city was a dull gray, common enough due to the dwarf's fixation on minerals. The noble's quarters and the castle, however, varied greatly in color. Minerals and metals ranging from obsidian to sandstone and steel to gold were layered on the sides of the houses. The larger the house meant more minerals used.

Gemstones also capped the corners and tops of some of the mansions, making them gleam in the light of the stars. Nauto could see a particularly large diamond on the top of the highest tower, which was positioned in the middle of the castle. The refracted and reflected light of the stars shining on the diamond, which the dwarves had even named Gemma, lit the castle, making the sight amazingly beautiful.

Nauto almost thought it a shame to make war in such a city. The battle would shatter the serenity of the shimmering city, destroying many precious metals and gems. It had to be done, sadly, if they were to win the Second Race War.

Astrum turned to face Nauto. "You must wait here until dawn, Nauto. It has been decreed that way by the gnomish king, Indoles." Nauto nodded in acceptance.

"My men have not rested for quite some time; that will be fine. If I may ask, why does the king not want us to proceed?" Nauto questioned, bemused.

Astrum tapped the side of his nose. "That is a secret, though you will see. For now, I must depart, and accompany the king once more. Wait until dawn, Nauto, but do not attack. Just wait. Vis, come here."

Vis obliged, and walked over to Nauto and Astrum. "You will be joining me, Vis. Come on, it will be fun."

On The Move

Astrum said, almost giddily.

Vis looked dubiously at Astrum, but accepted. With that, Astrum started to run back towards the gates, Vis close behind, leaving Nauto more perturbed than ever. He felt as though he would never figure Astrum out.

By the time Astrum had gotten back to Indoles, all the preparations were set, and dawn had nearly arrived. He told the king of his success in stopping the army's advance, and boarded one of the machines, along with Vis. Lamia and Silen boarded the same one as the king, while Gelu went on the third. Now all that was needed was the sun and the king's word.

"What do these contraptions do, Astrum?" Vis asked when he overlooked the machine from on top of it, on the deck.

Astrum simply smirked, but did not say a word.

The sun displayed its brilliance behind the machines, signaling that dawn had finally arrived in full. The gnomish king, in his loudest voice (which was not that loud), shouted, "We depart now!"

With his order, the machines were started, and Indoles' plan was put into full effect. With one stroke, he would avert all danger posed upon his people, as well as the dwarves.

Chapter 17

Acrophobia

Fifteen years earlier, Incendia quod Inculta

"Why does he still have wings?" a small dimidium child asked his father.

"Never mind that, son, move along." the father replied with slight disgust in his voice.

Vis looked at the father and son walking away, and sighed. He blew out a puff of highly pressurized air that was the breath weapon of green dragons. It hit the ground, creating a small cloud of sand. Every day he suffered veiled insults based upon his wings. For some reason, he had not had them removed at birth. He could not ask his parents why, for he had none. He was an orphan with no home. It was too late to remove the wings; it could only be done at birth. If at any other time they were cut off, the dimidium would die.

Vis had no friends, nor any other family. He had taken care of himself for the past ten years, which was when he found himself alone. He did not know who took care of him while he was a baby, but he survived after then by getting whatever food and shelter he could find.

Vis lived on the outskirts of Incendia quod Inculta, outside of the wall. It was the poor area of the city, and thieves were common. Vis was strong compared to other dimidium his age, as well as taller, despite his lack of good nutrition. He was able to overpower dimidium over twice his age, and by this he made his living; by ridding merchants of would-be thieves.

He carried with him a plain longsword, which was one of his rewards he received from getting rid of robbers for a blacksmith. It was slightly over half of his height, yet he wielded it easily in one hand. Everyone knew to stay away from Vis if they had evil intentions, for he would smite them down without mercy.

Vis looked up, and saw a dimidium running past him. Behind the dimidium was a well-known merchant, waving his hand in anger. The dimidium had obviously stolen some of his merchandise, and Vis started to chase after him, as well.

Vis, although tall for his age, could not catch up with the thief, and was slowly being left behind. The thief glanced back, a grin on his face.

In the moment that he looked back however, he accidentally ran into a cloaked figure. The thief was knocked down, while the cloaked person did not move in the slightest. Vis slowed to a stop, and watched the scene unfold.

The mysterious figure looked down upon the thief, who was trying to get to his feet. He grabbed a package, supposedly what he had stolen from the merchant, and tried getting past the cloaked figure. In one swift movement almost too fast for the eye to see, the figure grasped his sword, pulled it free of its sheath, and bashed the thief's head with its broadside.

The thief dropped the package, and tottered around like a drunkard for a moment or two, before finally falling down, unconscious.

The figure sheathed his blade, and walked towards Vis. He said not a word, nor did he bother to give the package back to the merchant, who gave a breathless thank you, though the figure did not acknowledge it.

Vis stood still, admiring the speed and strength of the figure. Vis let him pass by, and as the figure did, Vis could feel his scales tingling. The power of the cloaked figure could be felt through the air, and Vis was sure he was capable of some sort of magick, though he had not known any dimidium could perform such feats. Despite being half-dragon, many dimidium could not perform in that capacity.

Excited at the prospect of talking to such a powerful dimidium, Vis followed him.

"Excuse me," Vis started.

The figure did not stop, nor did he turn around. Vis tried again. "Excuse me, sir?" he tapped the figure on his shoulder.

Whirling, the figure drew his sword and held it high, ready to strike. Vis stepped back, his hand shooting to his own sword. Some light crept into the figure's hood, and Vis could see that it was no dimidium, but a man. Not to be put out, Vis tried to talk to the man again.

Vis started talking at a fast pace. "I did not mean to alarm you, sir. I just wanted to say how incredible you are. If you need anything, just let me know, and I will do it for you. I would be honored to travel with you and follow you to wherever you want to go."

Eager both to please the man and to calm him down, Vis nearly rambled on. He meant every word he said though; if he could learn some of this man's secrets, he could become a better warrior.

The man silently stared at Vis, green eyes glinting within his hood. He did not speak, but instead sheathed his sword and started to walk away again. Vis did not try to stop him again, but followed him for some time.

Vis and the mysterious man walked through the main gates of the city, past the wall, and walked until they were nearly at the noble's quarters, which was surrounded by a large metal gate. In the center of the city Vis could see a black temple, which sent shivers down his spine, though he knew not what it was there for. The wealthy estates surrounded the temple. One of the mansions was home to the king, though Vis did not know which.

On the other side of the temple, Vis could see the volcanic side of the city, which was much hotter than the desert. The two rivers, the Ignis and the Unda, flowed in the same direction, and the path they each took was the exact opposite as the other. They flowed this way until they both reached the sea. Vis had rarely been this deep in the city, and he did not remember it all clearly, so he admired the view.

Suddenly, the man turned to his left, and walked into a building. Vis looked up at the sign of the building, and saw that it was a mercenary guild, which gave jobs to anyone who walked through its doors.

Vis followed the man in, excited at the prospect of possibly going on a job with the man. Could they guard a caravan together, or maybe travel to distant cities to vanquish terrifying beasts that are plaguing them? Vis had never left the city, but he never considered it a home, so he felt that now was as good a time as any to leave.

When he walked in, Vis spotted the man across the room, which was full of large dimidium searching for jobs. The man was staring at a board where various bounties were posted. Vis walked over to him and looked at some of the jobs people needed doing. Some were relatively simple tasks; finding their lost pets, or helping with organizing their shops. Others were more exciting, like guarding shops or killing monsters.

The man seemed fixated on one particular notice, though Vis could not be sure. The poster was one to slay a monster. It must have been terrifying, for they gave it a name, which was "Atrox".

Vis had never heard of the beast before, and they did not give a drawing of it. He looked at the location of the monster, and was surprised to see that it was at the top of Montis, the mountain present in the human realm. That was a long distance to travel to put a notice just for one monster. He looked at the bounty of the beast.

Vis gasped loudly. Everyone in the room literally stopped to look at him. His exhalation of surprise captured the attention of even the deafest mercenaries (those who had one or both of their ears removed forcibly by claws or the sword). All, that is, except for the cloaked figure. He simply took the notice from the board, neatly folded it up, and then put it in one of his cloaks inside pockets.

The man walked away, and the room resumed its usual level of boisterousness, going back to ignoring the larger-than-normal dimidium teen. Vis had never before seen such an amount for a monster bounty.

Did that...did that really say one million *gold pieces?!* Vis wondered.

Vis did not think anything could be worth that much. The bounty must have been put out by a noble or even a *king*. Since it was in the human realm, it must have been the human king. Vis turned around, and just barely caught sight of the mysterious man leaving the building. Hurriedly, Vis followed him.

Vis left the guild, and searched for the man. Vis saw him a little way down the main road of the city. He started to run to catch up. Once he did, he walked beside the cloaked man.

"Uh, sir?" Vis started. The man made no sign of acknowledgment, but Vis continued anyway. "I think that may be too terrible a monster, if I may say so, sir. And, uh, sir, what is your name?" again, the man did not reply. "Do you mind if I call you by the name of the monster on that bounty?" Vis asked.

When the man failed to reply for the third time, Vis

gave up, and began to call the mysterious man by the name "Atrox"

From the base of the mountain, Vis could not see the top. It seemed to pierce the clouds, impaling the sky with its snow-capped point. Mount Montis was the tallest mountain in all of Solum, despite not being a part of any chain of other such mountains. It seemed ludicrous that something so colossal could exist in an otherwise flat terrain.

Vis glanced at Atrox to see if he could gauge his reaction to the immense mountain. Atrox was not even looking at it, but was instead walking towards it. Not once on their entire journey did Atrox speak. He did not make any type of sound, such as a grunt of acknowledgement if Vis talked to him. His lack of words was inversely proportional to his fighting capabilities, however.

Everything they had come across, whether it was sand wyrms, sand worms (gigantic flesh-eating burrowers), goblins, or any other sort of beast or monster, was defeated by Atrox. He was an unstoppable force of steel and magick.

Vis, on the other hand, had barely helped Atrox with killing any of the beasts. Not that he was not able to help, just that Atrox did not give him enough time to, not that the man needed any to begin with. Atrox never received any wounds, as he was too quick with the sword to get any.

Vis started to follow Atrox. There lay a small path

that lead up to the top, and that was the quickest route available. Even so, the trek would take a long time, as the path had many twists and turns, doubled-back on itself several times, and the distance to the top itself was immeasurable.

Vis started to make his way up the path, but was stopped by Atrox. Atrox raised his hands, and the mountain began to shudder. The sound of rocks crumbling and falling was a slight noise compared to the churning of the rocky landscape. The path that ran up Montis began to quiver, and the snake-like route straightened out. Atrox was not done, however. The path began to sprout stairs, as well, and soon enough the path had turned into the longest staircase Vis had ever seen.

The shuddering of the mountain stopped, and all grew still. Far above them, Vis could hear a loud roar, presumably the monster "Atrox" from the bounty. The roar itself made the mountain shake slightly, though not as much as it had been before. The beast must have been annoyed at the sudden and unexpected change of the mountain.

Atrox started walking up the steps, Vis close behind. It took them slightly over two hours to reach a point that was almost at the top of the mountain. It would have taken much longer had Atrox not made the stairs.

The higher they traveled, the more Vis became uncomfortable. He was not afraid of heights, but the air seemed to be very thin close to the peak of Montis. Atrox did not seem affected by it in the slightest, as always.

The only reason Vis did not pass out due to the lack

of breathable air was due to being a green dimidium. His lungs were constructed differently from other dimidium's, as green ones needed to be able to breathe out the compressed air with greater force than normal. His lungs were more akin to a bird's; unidirectional, meaning all the air that passed through his lungs was "fresh". All of the colored dimidium had a certain biological trait that was only possessed by one color, not including scale color itself.

Atrox stopped at the top of the stairs, causing Vis to nearly run into him. The top of the mountain was not a point, but flattened. Rocks jutted out of the wide, snowy space. More alarming were the amount of bones strewn about the area. Some were the bones of animals, but the majority was skeletons of humans. Now Vis knew why the bounty had been placed on the monster, and why it was so high; it had been killing and consuming humans, though not necessarily in that order.

Vis was suddenly buffeted by a large gust of wind. It was so strong it had knocked him down. Wind continued to pin him to the ground, but then it suddenly stopped. He sat up, and saw what had been creating the fierce wind.

It was griffon, a beast with the body of a lion but the head and wings of an eagle. Its eyesight was largely renowned across the world, as well as its ferocity in battle. Vis had seen several pass over Incendia quod Inculta, but they had never landed, nor did he imagine them so large when close up. The griffon must be the so called "Atrox".

The griffon squawked loudly in challenge, but Atrox the man did not move. He did not draw his sword, nor raise his hands to cast a spell. He stood there, motionless in front of the griffon. Vis did not understand what he was doing, why he did not attack. Surely he must do something against the beast? Vis drew his own sword in defense, though it seemed puny compared Atrox the man's sword, and even more so when compared to the size of the griffon.

Vis then realized something horrifying. Before, after Atrox the man had created the stairs, a loud roar occurred afterwards. A roar, not the squawking of a griffon. This monster could not have made such a sound, so that would mean...

A giant claw hit the ground in front of Vis, completely crushing the griffon underneath it.

"Silence, pest," a deep voice commanded, purring softly. A small squawk of pain was let out from the griffon, and then it became quiet.

Now Atrox the man drew his sword to face the real Atrox the monster, which was no griffon. It was a *divum*.

It was a beast usually found in the mountains of the dwarves, not the human's realm. It had the wings and back of a raven, and the front and head of a panther, and was sentient as well. It was both furred and feathered, and quite large, to say the least.

The divum was capable of destroying entire towns, as well as griffons, apparently. The species numbers had dwindled over the years, so it was strange to find one on the top of Montis, but not important enough to where Vis would ponder it for long. It turned its head in their direction.

"Disappear, vermin." Atrox the divum spoke,

hissing like a cat, furthering the terror of Vis. But not of Atrox the man, of course. He pulled out his sword and began to walk slowly towards the monster, with the intent to kill. The divum laughed, which was an odd combination of a raven's call and a panther's purr, then it reared up and buffeted them with its wings.

The force of the wind was so much stronger than that of the griffons that Vis was caught off-guard, and blown backwards. The wind caught on his wings, and pushed him off of the mountain.

Everything seemed to slow to a stop. The divum still reared up. Atrox the man turned around slowly. He looked at the falling dimidium.

Vis saw Atrox the man's eyes glow a bright green, for but a second. Vis felt a slight tingling in his body. Atrox the divum pounded the ground with its two front paws, returning to an animal position. Atrox the man faced away from Vis. He sprinted towards the divum, and jumped in the air, sword held high above his head.

Time resumed. Vis saw nothing more of Atrox the man or the divum, and he fell off the mountain, propelled outward by the force of the divum's wings. He had no time to think, let alone scream. He felt something quiver slightly on his back, and he closed his eyes.

Atrox the man stood over the decapitated body of Atrox the divum. He wiped his sword on the fur of the monster, and then sheathed it. He looked over the body once more, and then, without hesitation, ran off the edge of the mountain, and plummeted below.

Vis woke up with a gasp as the loud sound of cracking rocks echoed off of the mountain. He sat up, shivering, the fright of the fall still with him. He looked in front of him, and he saw Atrox the man, calmly walking towards him. Behind him was a large crater in the ground. Vis did not know what had happened at all. All he knew was that he would never travel so high ever again.

And he kept his promise to himself for fifteen long years, traveling with Atrox throughout that entire time, until that one fateful day when everything changed for Vis, forever.

Chapter 18

Mysteries Solved

Present time, Iugosus

"Hey...Astrum." Vis started, sounding slightly queasy.

Astrum looked over at him. The dimidium was looking slightly green, and not just because of his scales. He was holding on to the railing, and did not show any sign of taking the possibility of letting go. Astrum smirked, and walked over to Vis.

Astrum patted Vis on the back. Vis lurched forward a bit and groaned softly. "Y-you never told me," Vis gulped. "You never t-told me we would be d-doing this...*Atrox*."

Astrum gazed at Vis intently. He had not been called by that name ever since Vis knew what his true name was. Although it did make sense, for Vis was stressed, and part of the reason *was* Astrum himself. He was the one who told Vis to come along, because he thought it would get Vis over his fear of heights.

Instead, Vis seemed to revert back to his old typecast; a dimidium who blindly relied on a man he did not fully understand. Traveling with Astrum all that time did not change the fact that Vis was still scared.

Ah, well, Astrum thought, *perhaps he will never get over it.*

Nauto had become agitated. He crossed and uncrossed his arms, tapped his foot, and swayed slightly from side to side. The sun had come up slightly, and the mountain cast a great shadow upon the army of elves and humans. Astrum had said to wait until dawn, and he had, yet nothing happened. His only consolation was the fact that the dwarves had not done anything yet, either, though they must know by now that an army was waiting outside, ready to strike.

Nauto's troops were also becoming restless. They shuffled slightly in their armor, murmuring to each other. Nauto looked at the two who stood by him on each side.

Ferinus had sat down, and was aimlessly playing with a piece of his fur on his leg. Lex had not moved. She stood stoic and tall and did not budge at all. She was staring at the city, though Nauto could not gauge her emotions.

More time passed, and there was no response from

Astrum or the dwarves, so Nauto kept waiting. The sun rose steadily, bathing more of the army in its light as it did so. The light off the sun hit the diamond placed on the top of the castle, and light filled the entirety of the plains. The diamond, Gemma, made it so that light came earlier for the city, so the mountain would not prevent the dwarves from sleeping too late. It doubled as the dwarves' most valuable treasure, as well. They held the gem in higher esteem than the king, as it was of the purest quality, and held no flaws, as well as being quite humongous.

Suddenly, the light of the sun reflecting off of the diamond was obscured.

Three bulbous...*things* rose above the mountain, and came in between the sunlight and Gemma, the diamond. The army stopped its shuffling and mutterings to stare at the fantastic sight.

Nauto peered intently at the things floating in the sky. They each appeared to be a ship, since they had a flat top like a deck, and had round underbellies. The brightness of the sun prevented Nauto from making out much more, and he was not sure whether to be wary or joyful. Were these enemies as well, or the cavalry?

Something was dropped from the top of each of the floating ships. It was several long ropes, and it seemed that each of the ropes had a small figure dangling from it. In total there were nine ropes, three from each of the things (ships?) flying in the air. Each of the groups of three was holding something in between them. It looked like they were each holding a third of a large circle.

The groups on the left and the right started to swing towards the middle. It had the appearance of a high-altitude acrobatics act. They soon met the group in the middle, and connected to them by the things they were carrying. They dropped in height a bit, until they were right over the diamond of the dwarves.

Each of the groups dropped on top of the diamond, the top of it providing ample space for the nine figures, who appeared to be gnomes. They attached the circle thirds around the edge of the diamond, and then stood in the center of the gem.

The three floating ships started to rise higher, and with them came the diamond. The tower it once rested upon crumbled slightly around the rim where the gem was removed. The gnomes had constructed a circle that went around the diamond, and was able to lift it into the air, with the help of the flying ships.

Nauto saw the plan of the gnomes, now. To avoid battle, they would steal the prized diamond of the dwarves, Gemma, and then force them to surrender so they could retrieve it. It was a brilliant plan that reduced the cost of war on both sides, as well as sparing a beautiful city from destruction.

At that moment, when the diamond was safe within the gnomes' hands, there appeared other things in the sky from the north.

At that moment, the thought of a battle without destruction vanished.

Silen peered over the railing at the bow of the flying machine. It was only at that point and the back of the ship that afforded a view of what was under the vessel.

The large balloon underneath the mechanical ship prevented anything from seeing past it down below on the sides, but the deck of the ship protruded outward past the front and back of the balloon.

Below him, Silen saw the city, which seemed to grow smaller and smaller the farther down he looked. The castle was right in front of him, but the lower parts of the city were distant. Silen sighed contently; he never imagined he could see a sight such as this.

The airship, which Indoles had named them, was magnificent. The ability to move while flying was due to an engine that the king himself designed, which took the form of a mechanized propeller on the stern of the airship that could move from side-to-side, allowing the airship to turn mid-flight. It ran without the aid of any being, instead running on a type of crystal which produced its own energy, which the king had called "Sustineo".

Lamia was peering off into the distance off of the stern of the airship, and she called Silen over. He walked over to her, and she pointed towards the horizon. Past the other airship, Silen saw more mountains on the horizon, as well as Praecingo ocean, but one particular one caught his attention.

"It is peculiar, right, Silen?" Lamia asked. Silen nodded his head.

The mountain in question was unlike any of the others. Instead of being a light gray, it was instead a jet black. Also, it did not seem to be rugged like a mountain, either, but very sleek. It was slightly smaller than the mountains near it, but it was still very large.

"That would be Cornu Mountain," Indoles remarked,

sidling up next to them. "The dwarves have tried to mine from it, but it is made out of a very hard substance, and their equipment was unable to even chip it. We gnomes have studied it for some time, but still do not know what it truly is."

Silen's eyes widened at the thought of such an impenetrable mountain existing. It seemed like an immovable object, even more so than any other mountain.

They heard yelling from the port side of the airship, and they turned their attention that way. Silen, Lamia, and King Indoles gasped as one. All at once, the hope that they had each held for the gnome's plan fell as they saw what flew rapidly towards them.

A horde of dragons glided and roared in the distance, dozens upon dozens of the scaled monstrosities, in their many different sizes and colors, all soaring towards the ship with malicious intent.

Silen kept his eyes on the dragons that were swiftly approaching them. At the front of the large force of dragons was one slightly larger than the rest. A figure was mounted on this one, and appeared to be directing the dragons. The force of dragons split up into three groups; one group for each of the flying machines.

One dragon flew ahead of the group, overly eager. A bolt of lightning streaked out of its yellow maw, piercing the balloon of the ship to the left of the one Silen was on.

The balloon exploded instantaneously, and the deck of the machine rose, and thunderously cracked in two, in tandem with the sound of the thunder that accompanied the lightning. Wooden planks splintered and shattered, the debris hitting Silen's own airship, but not enough to puncture their balloon. Everything began to tumble to the ground, including the ship's passengers.

Several larger dragons immediately fell upon the yellow dragon, rending its wings and body. Apparently the leader of the dragons did not want the airships to be harmed, for a reason Silen did not understand. At least the other two airships seemed to be safe for now.

Then he remembered. Both Astrum and Vis were on that airship. Silen was not worried for Astrum, but Vis was surely in danger.

"VIS!" Silen yelled at the top of his lungs, hoping that Astrum could save the dimidium somehow.

"Astrum!" Vis shouted. "Wake up!"

Astrum opened his eyes slowly, and rubbed them. He stretched and yawned, and peered around.

He stood up quickly, realizing that an ambush by dragons should not be slept through. Astrum glanced at Vis, whose terror of heights seemed to be forgotten for the moment.

The lightning struck, a loud eruption of noise occurred, and Vis and Astrum were thrown off of the airship. They spun through the air, flying apart from each other. Astrum tried to reach out to grab Vis, but they were too far apart. Vis drifted away from him, and then in the chaos he lost sight of the dimidium.

Astrum then focused on trying to stop spinning in the air. He balanced himself, and saw that the some of the dragons had moved past the destroyed machine. One of the dragons passed underneath him, and he grabbed onto one of the spikes of its back as it did so.

The white dragon turned its neck around to look at Astrum, and snapped at him. It was a medium-size dragon, but Astrum was still able to bat its head away. He grabbed onto the point where its wings met its body, and quickly gained control over the dragon's flight. Astrum searched for Vis, but could not spot him amongst the falling debris and gnomes.

Astrum glanced behind him at the remaining two ships. The dragons were attacking them, but did not destroy them. The weight of the diamond carried by the two airships had brought them down, but they did not sink to the ground. The two airships did, however, move closer together because of the diamond, to the point where they almost crashed into each other. The gnomes onboard were able to correct the problem, however, and turned the airships opposite directions from each other.

Astrum flew the dragon he was on to the leader of the group of dragons. He had recognized that gray clothing, as well as the blue glint of the sword of the figure standing upon the back of the large dragon, and knew what he had to do to stop the advance of the dragons.

Vis fell through the air at an alarming rate. He had not bothered to balance himself in the air, and instead just let the wind spin his body about. The air rushing past his head made him deaf to all other things, and his mind was surprisingly lucid.

Oddly, he was immensely calm. His fear of heights had fled him, and he found himself thinking of his time spent with Astrum. They had traveled most of Solum, defeating monsters and guarding treasures as mercenaries for hire. Astrum did not care for the money that was offered to them, so the only time Vis would eat was when they were paid beforehand to carry out the task. He could have become rich when they defeated Atrox the divum, but they never went to the client who had put out the bounty.

Vis then thought of his time spent with the group. Sometime during then, Astrum had finally started to talk, and Vis found himself admiring the immortal even more. He was witty and confident, but almost nothing he said was without a deeper meaning.

Vis remembered Astrum's parting words to him when he went on his quest to find out about Neque. "How a bird could fly if it was too scared to do so?"

Vis chuckled, realizing that the answer to the simple question was simple in itself. The bird must simply unfold its wings and force itself to fly, else it will not survive. How else could a bird hunt or travel?

Inspiration struck Vis. He balanced himself, and then dove towards the ground. He willed his wings to open, realizing that he had done the same when he had fallen off the mountain.

It was not Astrum who had saved Vis, it was he himself who had!

His wings unfolded, their span reaching wider than he was tall. Vis plunged farther, traveling parallel to the city on the mountain. He reached the base of the mountain, and used his breath weapon, which being a green dimidium was highly compressed air, to launch himself back into the sky.

Vis flew straight up, until he reached the height where gravity would start to pull him back to the ground. He flapped his wings, and stayed aloft. He laughed heartily, and then gently dropped to the ground. He no longer had any need to fear heights, for he could conquer them. His phobia was cured.

When he touched the ground, Vis knelt down for a moment, contemplating what had just occured. Vis grasped the handle of the two-handed sword he carried, and unsheathed it. He stood up tall, gazing at its keen edge. Vis smiled at his reflection on the blade. He looked behind him, and saw the army some way off. They seemed to still have their attention on the events occurring in the sky.

Vis turned his focus to it as well. He crouched down, and then exploded off of the ground with the help of his breath weapon, launching himself into the air to join in the fight. He was not about to miss it so easily.

Nauto stood amazed. He could not move a muscle. So many things had happened at once that he did not know what to do. He had seen the fall of the flying ship, and he saw a figure take control over one of the dragons. That could only be Astrum, as Nauto knew now one else who would think of doing such a thing while plummeting through the air. He had also seen another figure that glinted green as he fell. It had flown safely to the ground, and then rejoined the battle in the sky. That could only be Vis, though he had not known that the dimidium could fly.

Nauto shook his head to clear his mind. He looked back at the two flying ships, and saw that the dragons had severed the ropes that carried the diamond. The shining brilliance of the gem blinded Nauto for a moment, but then it fell into the city, crushing a mansion beneath it completely.

That was the army's hope of not having to fight, but it seemed that it was lost. Nauto turned around to look at his troops, who were all in awe of the aerial battle. He took a deep and long breath.

"CHARGE! WE TAKE IUGOSUS NOW!" Nauto thunderously roared, and then sprinted towards the city.

His troops had jumped slightly, but heeded his words well. They surged forward behind him, filled with adrenaline and the thought of victory.

Chapter 19

Clashing Forces

Gelu shot to his feet after he heard the explosion. He ran across the deck of the airship to see the flaming wreck of what was once a similar airship falling on the city of Iugosus. Gelu cursed as he saw the perpetrators of the act, which was a veritable group of dragons. More were approaching from the back of the airship he was on.

Gelu was thrown to his feet. The airship had suddenly jolted upwards slightly. He ran to the front of the airship to see diamond, Gemma, falling to the city. He cursed again, and he unsheathed his claws. He had sent his men to protect the gnomes still on the ground, and so he was to be the only one able to truly protect the airship he was on. Although, without the diamond, the airships had become useless.

Gnomes were scurrying around the deck, though they seemed calm. They brought up two machines from below the deck, which had a limited amount of storage. They had the appearance of smaller catapults, but seemed completely mechanized. The gnomes loaded the machine with a medium-sized rock, and one pulled a lever as a dragon passed by.

With enormous force, the rock shot forward, hitting the dragon directly on the side of its head. It fell to the city, knocked unconscious. Gelu laughed at the dragon, who had been bested by the technology of the gnomes. Gelu had his own thought then, and though it was insane, it seemed like it was the only way he would get to be in the action.

He sprinted to one of the catapults, and jumped on, ignoring the protests of the gnomes. Gelu kicked the lever back, and the machine sprung him out into the open sky. The air whipped past his face as he hurdled towards the other airship. Below him he saw dragons flying to attack the city. It seemed the dragons' goal was to destroy as much as they could. He landed on the deck of the other airship, and rolled slightly to decrease his momentum.

At the back of the ship he saw Silen and Lamia, both fighting the dragons. Silen threw his daggers at the dragons, scoring some hits, and then calling his weapons back to him. It was an unorthodox way to fight, but it worked better than close-combat. Lamia was busy shouting out words of magick and using the appropriate spell components to make them work. One of the dragons was suddenly caught up in a spider's web, while another was lanced with beams of light. The combination of the two fighting was deadly and effective, even against dragons.

A dragon flew over his head, flying back towards the others of its kind. On the dragon's back he saw Astrum holding onto its wings, apparently steering the monster. Gelu chuckled once more; the battle was insane.

The airship lurched forward slightly. Gelu looked behind him to see that one of the smaller dragons had landed. The color of its scales was a light tan, a color Gelu had not seen before on a dragon. Though, by the color, he could guess what it would be.

The dragon opened it mouth wide, and out came a miniature sandstorm, as Gelu expected. The deck of the ship was pelted with sand, and instantly became weathered. Gelu dodged the majority of the sand, and was able to keep his footing on the tilting airship.

Several gnomes ran in front of Gelu, and set up some sort of machine that looked nothing like the catapult he had seen before. It appeared to be an ordinary box with holes, capable of doing nothing. They aimed it towards the dragon, and pushed a small button on the side of the machine.

Springing forth from the box was a large multitude of arrows. They all hit the dragon, several piercing its underside, while one scored a hit in one of its eyes. The dragon rolled onto its side, and fell off of the machine, roaring in pain and anger.

"Damn it all, I want to fight!" Gelu shouted, exasperated.

The wall surrounding the base of the mountain was left unguarded, which Nauto thought was odd. Even if it was a trap, however, the army still needed to invade, so they surged through the gates of the city.

Just past the wall were three colossal staircases, which had two equally large caves in between them. Nauto turned to face Lex.

"You take the stairs and clear out the city; I will take my men and clear the underground." Nauto commanded. Lex nodded, and waved her hand in the direction of the stairs. She charged up them with half of the army following her.

Nauto and Ferinus unsheathed their weapons, and lead the other half of the army into the darkness of the tunnels. Cruor was able to remove his shroud as they traveled deeper into the mountain, and strode alongside Nauto. Being so close to the vampire sent chills down his spine, but it was nothing like before, when he had first met him.

They traveled deeper down the tunnel until it opened into a large cavern. There were more houses, but they were nothing like the ones outside. Instead of being square, the designs were much more ludicrous. Some houses were pyramids, while others were spheres. All seemed to have some sort of mechanical device on them, and Nauto realized that the gnomes must live inside the mountain.

The army traveled through the urban area, and reached an area past them. It was a wide open space, and beyond it were three great bridges that lead over a huge abyss. Across them was the lower part of the castle. Underground, the castle seemed to extend even farther, rather than having supports. This part of the castle must be where the king of the gnomes ruled.

Across the chasm, just before the castle, was another wide space. The dwarven army had amassed there. Clad in armor, the dwarves were ready to war. Their armor was bulkier than the elves, but that closed the gap that the elves' agility created. They wielded weapons ranging from hammers to axes to swords. Despite their lack of height, the dwarves were excellent in handling large weapons, and could easily overcome their foes.

The dwarves were an honorable race however, and would resort to no trickery, so Nauto felt the fight would be as fair as any fight could be. The numbers of the two forces seemed to be similar. He quickly formulated a plan. The best way to fight the dwarves would be to travel across the three bridges and meet them halfway, before they could reach the side Nauto was on.

Nauto turned around. "We travel across the bridges! Do not let the dwarves pass them!" he shouted.

The elves raised their arms into the air, shouting their compliance. Nauto ran to the center bridge, his army breaking off into thirds. Veneratio led his human contingent as well as a third of the elves up the left bridge, while Ferinus traveled to the right bridge.

As they reached the bridges, and started to make their way across them, Nauto noticed something peculiar. The dwarves did not seem to be moving, and instead stood their ground, watching the elven force run towards them. The closer Nauto got to the end of the bridge, the lower his heart sank. His courage turned to horror as he realized the dwarves were not dwarves at all, but were instead mannequins set up in armor to look like dwarves.

Nauto did not stop running, as he was sure that staying on the bridge would be fatal. There was some movement in the fake army. A dwarf appeared in front of the ranks of mannequins, and in his hand he held something small and silvery. He smiled evilly, and pushed something on what he held in his hand.

Veneratio looked across the bridges. He felt uneasy traveling across them, for some unknown reason. He must follow Nauto, however, for he was a great elf. The elf was a prince, yet he seemed more like an adventurer. He was fearless in battle, and a great strategist. Still, Veneratio could not shake the feeling of animosity emanating from the other side of the rift where the dwarven army was.

He rushed across the bridge, followed by a third of the army. Across the bridge, the dwarves did not budge. At this point, they should have met the elven/human army halfway, for they were divided, and would be easier to defeat.

There was movement among the ranks of the still dwarves. One dwarf stepped away from the crowd, and smiled. He held something in his hand, but Veneratio could not make out what it was. The dwarf raised his hand, and pressed down on the object.

Veneratio's world was razed by an inferno of devilry.

Clashing Forces

The bridge to the left of Nauto exploded in a great fire. The cavern shook as the bridge blew apart. Pieces of debris and elven bodies flew into the air from the force of the explosion, and then fell into the chasm. The screams of his comrades reached Nauto's ears. Their anguished cries grew softer as they plunged down into the dark void.

Veneratio, as well as a third of his army, had been destroyed within an instant. Nauto turned his gaze away from the horror, and focused on the dwarf who had caused the explosion. The dwarf stood there dumbly, holding the device in his hands. He pressed the button again, and Nauto feared another explosion, but none occurred.

Nauto sprinted to the dwarf, filled with rage. The dwarf, now frightened, dropped the detonator and started to run, but he could not flee. Nauto ran him through with his rapier, and stood there a moment, completely still, the dwarf twitching slight upon his blade.

Sighing greatly, he removed his sword from the dwarf's body, which slumped to the ground. Nauto wiped the blood off his blade on the dead body, and sheathed it.

Cruor sidled next to him, and picked up the dwarven corpse. He sank his fangs deep into the dwarf's neck, sucking out the blood.

Nauto turned around, disgusted, and grieved for his fallen comrades. They had been lucky that the other bridges had not done the same, though that seemed to be due to a malfunction in the machine that the dwarf used. He had not known dwarves could use such deception in war. Nauto mourned silently, and made his way through the army of dwarven mannequins.

Lex traveled up the stairs, followed by both men and elves. She had gotten used to constant running and fighting during the war, as well as commanding her men. As she charged up the staircase, she thought of the time when she was an archer holding the pass through Mount Montis. There would be no intervention of a godly fighter like Astrum here, she hoped. Umbra did not want to fight Lumen, just as she did not want to fight him, so they stayed in their respective lands.

She noticed something strange about the city. It seemed to be desolate, with no sign of the dwarves anywhere. Dragons ravaged the upper city and the castle, but did not bother her army, yet. Hopefully they would thin out the dwarves, wherever they might be.

Suddenly, the ground shook. It did not last long, but it caught Lex off-guard. She stopped momentarily to wonder what caused the mountain to shake, but let it go. She must clear out the city.

"Onwards!" Lex shouted at the army, who had also stopped at the beginning of the shaking. They were in the merchant's area now, but there were still no dwarves around. Lex started to feel a sense of unease as she traveled farther up the city.

Clashing Forces

Vis flew through the air, exultant. Flying upwards with just his wings was slow going, but with the aid of the highly pressurized air he could breathe, and he could soar in an instant. He was careful to avoid the dragons, for though he could fly, he would be no match for the much larger beasts.

Vis flew until he reached the deck of the airship that Lamia and Silen were on. He spotted them on the stern of the ship, fending off the dragons. The alacer that Astrum had told him about, Gelu, was also trying to fight, but with little effect. He would be deadly, if only he could reach the dragons, but his claws were lacking in that respect.

Vis held his sword out before him, ready to attack those who came too close to the airship. Oddly, no dragon truly attacked the ship. It seemed they were using guerrilla warfare, which was attacking swiftly, and retreating much the same. They did no real damage to the airship, and Vis did not know what to make of it. They had destroyed the other airship with little effort, yet did not do so to the others.

He looked beyond to see the leader of the dragons. Instead of there being one dragon rider, there were now two. Vis recognized that Astrum was the second rider, and he seemed to be talking to the other rider. That changed, however, as they unsheathed their swords and leapt at each other, clashing midair, their swords shining brightly, one green, one blue.

Silen turned around, ceasing his attacks on the dragons momentarily. He spotted Vis on the deck, looking around.

He ran over to Vis. "Vis! I am glad to see you are all right."

Silen patted Vis on the shoulders, and Vis responded by unfolding his wings to their full length. Silen stepped back, astonished, but then smirked. "I guess it was not Astrum who saved you, then." His smile fled from his face, however, as he realized something important.

"Vis, do you think you could carry a passenger? I have an idea," Silen asked.

Vis stared at Silen dubiously, but nodded his head. "I should be able to carry one, yes."

Silen turned around to look at Lamia. "Lamia!" he shouted. She turned her head slightly to glance back at Silen.

"I will return shortly, hold the airship, all right?!" Not questioning him, she nodded her head slowly, and resumed her spells. She seemed to be slumped over slightly, however; hopefully she had the energy to continue on a bit longer.

Gelu walked over to the pair. "What is happening?" Silen laughed, and put his hand on Gelu's shoulder.

"You will see. Could you do something for me? I would like you to protect Lamia, just in case. Could you do that for me?" Silen asked, his demeanor turning serious. Gelu nodded, confusion plastered on his face.

"Good. Let us go, Vis." Without a moment's

hesitation, Silen ran to the edge of the airship and jumped off. Vis quickly followed him, unfolding his wings once again. He dove towards Silen, and caught him. The added weight was not as much as Vis had anticipated, meaning the flight would be easier than he would have thought.

"Where to, Silen?" Vis asked.

Silen laughed. "To see he who is ruling the dwarves. To the castle!"

"It does not have to be this way."

"Oh, I am afraid it does. You see, the land has been taken over by those who do not care for it. They indiscriminately build cities and ravage the land for its resources. Even the elves are guilty of this, nature-loving as they are."

"They made the continent to what it is today. Many of their own lives have been lost as a result, and doing this has not been without certain sacrifices. Why destroy all they have worked for?"

"I have ruled the dragons ever since I disposed of their king. They grew to share my sentiments, however. In return for their loyalty, I will do what we both desire. The balance of the world must be kept to how it was before the races invaded its sanctity. You who sympathize with them cannot hope to understand."

"You are right, I do not understand. Thousands of years ago when they came, they fought with the dragons, who had lived here long before, and I put an end to it, making them live in peace. Do the dragons still hold their grudge, after all this time?"

"Of course."

"I see no further use in talking. Let us end this between ourselves, Neque."

"If we must, Astrum."

Nauto and Cruor ran up the many flights of stairs to the top of the castle. He had posted his men outside, along with Ferinus, to guard the entrance. Nauto and Cruor had not met with any opposition since entering the castle, and the higher they traveled, the more the sense of dread grew in him. There was nothing they could do but confront the dwarven king, Adamans, and find out what was happening.

They went up many sets of stairs, the kingdom gradually changing color. The gnomish interior was full of machines and great cogs and gears. The dwarven interior was of metal and minerals, making the walls appear to be a vast amount of different colors, opacities, and textures.

They traveled up one last set of stairs, and arrived in a large hall. The floor had a long red carpet on it, leading to two large doors. A single window was in the ceiling, which made the corridor dark save for a beam of light that lit the center of the room.

The king must reside beyond, Nauto thought as he started to walk down the corridor. The walls were studded with grand gemstones of every color, but none were nearly the same size as the Gemma diamond that had sat atop the castle.

"Nauto!" a voice shouted from behind him and Cruor. It was Lex, clad in armor, sword unsheathed.

After greetings were made, Lex explained the situation in the city. She met with no force of dwarves whatsoever, and was worried of the fact. She had left her soldiers outside to guard the plaza that was before the castle doors.

As she stopped talking, a great shattering of glass occurred overhead. Glass rained down upon them like sharp rain. Through the large window that was on the ceiling of the corridor came Vis and Silen, flying down to join the group.

"Hello, Nauto! Lex!" Vis shouted from above. He laughed heartily. Nauto had never seen Vis as happy as he seemed now. He supposed flight would lift one's spirits immeasurably.

Together they walked down to the end of the hallway. They stopped at the double doors, which were made of pure gold. Nauto, Vis, Cruor, and Silen all pushed at once, opening both of the doors wide. They passed through them, all of their weapons at the ready. The room was darker than the hallway, though this gloom seemed unnatural.

Sitting upon throne, which was also made out of pure gold, sat a figure. He did not have the stature of a dwarf, but his clothes did appear to be of royalty.

Instead of his robes being a deep purple or blue, like that of any king's, they were pure black, as though night had taken them under its wing. Indeed it had, as from the figure's back grew two large, black wings. He laughed demonically, the echo of which traveled down the hall, making it seem as if his voice was all around them.

"I bid thee welcome, pawns." his deep voice seemed familiar to Nauto, and the realization of who it was sunk in quickly as the figure unsheathed a large, black blade that was a cruel as he was.

"Umbra." Silen and Cruor both hissed in fury.

Chapter 20

Malevolent Machinations

Silen had not forgotten the pain of losing not only his mother, but of his village. All his love and hard work had gone into improving their lifestyles. Lamia had helped to fill the void, but with the appearance of Umbra, all those feelings of animosity and rage came rushing back.

With no thought of his own safety, he lunged at Umbra, daggers held high. Their tips came down upon Umbra's sword, who laughed as he redirected Silen's strike as if it was child's play. To Umbra, however, it was. Cruor joined in on the fight, swinging his great sword in a wide arc towards Umbra's head. Silen recovered from Umbra's push, and came at him from below. Umbra laughed and met their strikes with his blade, at the same time. Cruor's sword was stopped by the hilt of Diabolus, Umbra's sword, while Silen's blades met the broadside of the sword.

Umbra let loose a dark pulse of magick that pushed them both back, shaking the room with its force. He licked the edge of his blade.

"This is the power you possess? Your rage does not compare to my own, mortals. Come at me with your full anger. I wish to taste its merciless kiss," Umbra crooned.

Nauto and Vis joined Cruor and Silen in attacking Umbra. Lex stood alone, shaking. It was to be like the mountain pass of Montis again, but this time she would not survive. The evocation of that time froze her muscles, as well as her mind. She could do nothing but watch the fruitless battle occurring right in front of her.

The four men could not overcome Umbra. Not Vis and Cruor with their brute strength, or Silen and Nauto with their dexterity. He was mightier and faster than the four combined, not to mention his proficiency with magick. Umbra parried, dodged, and retaliated to each of their strikes; no matter how well it was timed, or how synchronized with the attacks of the others.

Lex stared in utter dismay as her friends fought with the undefeatable. Did they not see how hopeless it was to go against this immortal fiend? Lex looked at her sword, quivering in her hands. It was not the sword that faltered, but her heart. Was she so weak? The deaths of her comrades would be the only thing she accomplished if she did not act, but still she could not find the strength to do so.

Astrum would scoff at her, if he was here. He would join in the fray, that feral expression on his face that seemed joyful at the same time. He, however, was immortal. She *could* die. Astrum had slain her fellow soldiers, and she did nothing to stop him. Lex gripped her sword.

Can I let them die in front of me, like I have before? Lex thought. Her life seemed insignificant in the face of the happiness that the group had given her. They had laughed and sang together, and Lex could not thank them enough for saving her from the fear that she once held.

She *must* help them. Resolution filled her soul, as well as her blade. Her trembling ceased, and she strode towards Umbra.

With the same fury that she held when she had struck Astrum on the *Ocean's Will* in the harbor of Monstrum, Lex screamed and ran forward, plunging her sword deep into Umbra's chest.

The fighting ceased. Silen, Nauto, and Vis all stared at Lex with surprise. Umbra stared at her sword which was stuck in his chest. Cruor yelled as well, swinging his sword towards Umbra's neck.

Cruor's sword connected, but it did not cut Umbra. No blood appeared from either wound, though both hits would have been grievous to anyone else. Umbra regarded Lex evilly.

"Yes!" Umbra roared, glee within his voice and the cruel smile upon his face once more. "This is the true power of fury! The rage blazes in you like the color of your hair! Let me share the sentiment and pleasure with you, my dear!"

The dark immortal thrust his blade forward, piercing Lex's armor. She choked as the blade slid into her. Warmth left her body, save for the searing steel that entered her chest.

Umbra leaned in close, and whispered in Lex's ear, "Seethe till the light fades, *Lex*."

She fell to the floor as Umbra removed his blade. She writhed in agony upon the ground, while Umbra snickered. He sheathed his sword and sprung wings from his back, unfurling them.

"I take my leave. Give my regards to Astrum." Umbra said. He laughed diabolically and took off.

"NO!" Silen shouted as Umbra soared away, shattering the single circular ceiling window to pass through. As he left the room, the abnormal darkness lifted, though the sun did not envelop the room completely, so Cruor was safe.

Silen slumped to his knees, and started to weep softly. Nauto sat down by Lex, and quickly removed her armor to examine her wound. Vis sat down in the dwarven king's chair, exhausted. Cruor raged around the room, breaking gemstones indiscriminately with his sword.

Nauto shook his head, as if to forget the events that just occurred. He looked over Lex, whose breathing had become very shallow. The sword wound had punctured a lung, if not both. No one could save her now. Nauto closed his eyes and whispered a small prayer, tears falling slowly from his eyes.

Cruor stopped his rampage, and regarded Lex carefully. Although she seemed to have passed, a heartbeat was still there, however faint. Cruor sighed heavily, and strode over to her. Before Nauto could protest, Cruor picked her head up and bit deep into her neck. Instead of drawing blood, however, he gave it. The feast he had on the dwarf before had sated his hunger; he did this to save Lex.

Nauto tried prying Cruor free of Lex, not realizing his intentions. After several moments of struggling, Nauto let go, just as Cruor did with Lex. He set her back down gently, and watched her closely.

Several more tense moments passed, and Lex's breathing returned to normal. The blood of a vampire could heal those near death. The drawback was that they, too, would become a vampire. Nauto stared at Lex in disbelief, still not comprehending what had transpired.

"She is as I am, now. For better or for worse, she will live. It will take her several days to wake however." Cruor whispered. "Keep her out of the light."

Nauto peered at Lex, not sure of whether to be joyful that she would live, or frightened that she would be like Cruor. Regardless, Nauto thanked Cruor for doing such a thing. Cruor simply shook his head, and left the room. At the doorway, he dropped his sword on the ground. It clattered loudly on the marble floor, cracking it with its weight. Nauto watched him walk into the corridor, opening his arms wide.

Cruor stepped into the light that filtered down through the window broken by Vis. Nauto jumped to his feet, and sprinted towards Cruor, who turned around, a sad smile on his face. He tilted his head slightly, but whether in pain or thanks Nauto did not know. Fire sprung from his body, the light of the sun burning Cruor.

"I bid thee farewell, Nauto. I shall be free of this coil. My journey was for naught, I suppose. That woman will take up the curse in my stead. I am weary, Nauto, drained of vitality. I cannot go on." Cruor said, and gazed up at the sun. Nauto stopped running, realizing the trials Cruor had gone through.

"The sun is so bright, a light I once fought. Now swallow me, night, free me from my thought." Cruor disappeared in a great flame, and all that remained was ash.

Nauto lamented the vampire's passing, brutal and insane as he was. There had been many losses this day, and they were all one-sided. The march against the dwarves seemed to be folly, now. Nothing had been accomplished, save the loss of many lives.

The two great beings watched the chess board intently. For little over three months now, they had been unable to control any piece on the board. This loss of manipulation had never before occurred, save for during the First Race War.

The "Lucidus" piece, along with a piece of pure white, one of pitch black, and one of gray had taken over the influence that the two great beings had over all other pieces, wreaking havoc over the board. They had received no command to try and stop this, either. They, simply, were at a loss.

Suddenly, a great bolt of lightning occurred over their heads, followed by the resounding crash of thunder. They peered upwards, knowing that He was coming. He would be the one to stop the destruction of the chess board.

"Do you," A voice from above boomed from the huge rift in the white ceiling that appeared, "wish to return, O Fallen Star?"

It paused shortly. "No, I perceive no recognition from you as of yet. You do not comprehend your true nature." He spoke in long, drawn-out syllables, his deep voice seeming to contain the depths of the universe itself.

His hand came down, and he waved it over the five-layered board. The box supporting the board opened, yet the board remained in place, floating. Inside the box was a large piece, nearly as large as the chess board itself. It seemed to be made out of crystal. It moved, seemingly of its own accord, but it was controlled by His will.

"You will return, one day. This will develop you, make you strong enough to face me once more, but will crush your hope. Hope, truly, is a mere illusion. It does not exist; not in the light, nor in shadow. Fear reigns supreme over all other emotions."

He laughed as the monstrous piece turned its head on the board. "Even time holds its own measure of fear."

Astrum stood tall. Neque and he had jumped from the backs of the dragons that they had ridden on, and fought throughout their descent. They reached the ground and fought more, though the battle between the two seemed to be endless.

They charged at one another once more. Their blades clashed together, the force of their strikes stronger than that of any other being. Each time their swords met, it was as if they attracted each other, like some magnetic force. Neque's face did not hold any ferocity, but kept its doleful expression throughout. Astrum snarled, and disengaged. He jumped back, and readied himself to charge again, but was stopped as the ground rumbled.

It seemed that it was an earthquake. The ground shook relentlessly, as if the world was to be turned over. Another sound was carried over the rumbling. It sounded like dragon's roar, but it was so loud that it was as if the dragon was right next to Astrum. Nothing could be so loud without being close enough to see, so Astrum thought. As loud as it was, however, it still seemed to be muted in some way, as if underwater.

Neque sighed, and walked towards Astrum, but passed by him. Astrum turned to look at what Neque saw. Beyond Iugosus and Mount Procerus there was something rising from the earth.

It appeared to be a black spike, but it was the size of a mountain. It rose above Procerus Mountain, and Astrum could see it was attached to something larger. Something that appeared to be made of an opaque, white crystal.

Something so monstrously colossal that it seemed that it could engulf the world whole.

Lamia was exhausted. The dragons seemed to keep coming endlessly, and she was running out of spell components. Gelu was able to fend off any dragon that got too close, but the fight was going against them.

Down below, Lamia started to hear a great rumble. It was as if a volcano had erupted in the vicinity, but she could see none. The dragons, however, as they heard the rumbling, seemed to grow panicked. They all gradually flew away, their roars turning to frightened mewls.

Lamia looked around in confusion. Then, off the stern of the ship, she saw Cornu Mountain rising from the ground. She stopped moving, completely shocked by the pure absurdity of what was happening. It was completely illogical to think that such a thing could move, much less rise. Lamia thought she was seeing some illusion, but Gelu confirmed its existence by letting out a small noise that sounded like he was choking.

The ground around the mountain broke apart, releasing its hold upon it. Underneath Cornu Mountain seemed to be something that it rode upon. It had the appearance of a very large diamond, though that was as huge an understatement as there had ever been. The more it rose, the larger Lamia realized it was.

Suddenly, however, it stopped, just when Lamia thought it could not get any bigger than it already was. The shuddering stopped, as did the destruction of the mountains around it. The landscape had been completely desolated around where the mountain had once been. Mountains, trees, rivers, all destroyed and replaced with an immensely over-sized gem.

Then, halfway in between the ground and Cornu Mountain, on the face of the crystal, something opened. Lamia gasped when she realized that what was opening was none other than an eye. This thing that ascended from the ground was some sort of beast, and Cornu Mountain had been its horn. Far out to the ocean, Lamia could see another mountain that was as black as pitch as the other.

The great eye of the beast peered around, slowly observing the land. As it looked upon the land, Lamia realized something horrifying. If it was as gigantic as it seemed, then the amount of its head that was showing was not the entirety of it.

The eye closed, as suddenly as it had opened, and all became still. The dragons had long since fled, and the airships made little to no sound. Lamia did not think it was quite yet over, however.

With the sound of a thousand explosions, the rest of the head tore free of the ground, further decimating the land. Luckily, it was still some distance away, so Procerus was not destroyed as the other mountains had been, but rocks and other debris fell on the deck of the airship, pelting it like hailstones. The immense head seemed to float in the air, but it was simply that its neck was not visible, as it was still largely under the ocean of Praecingo.

It turned its gaze on the airships. The wind shifted suddenly, and the airships were blown sideways. The gnomes on the airship had not frozen as Lamia and Gelu had, but instead tried to increase the speed of the airships via the machines below decks, so to get away from the creature, which appeared to be a dragon.

The dragon snorted. Two large smoke clouds issued from its nostrils, and it billowed down and outward into the mountain range. The smoke reached Procerus Mountain, and enveloped it whole, as it did with every other mountain in the vicinity. Lamia looked towards the ground, but could not see anything, save for the very tips of the mountains.

Next, the dragon breathed in. Its deep inhalation created a great suction, and it pulled the two airships backwards. Indoles and the other gnomes frantically tried to get away, but the pull was too strong. After a moment or so, the monstrosity stopped, and was still once more. The airships started to move again, but had been pulled back to over the top of Mount Procerus.

Lamia dreaded the next few moments. This drago was capable of destroying everything within the mountain range with one flick of its tail, one swipe of its claw. What was it doing? Lamia feared whatever its breath weapon would turn out to be. She had never before seen a dragon whose skin was like a diamond, so she had no idea what kind of substance it could exhale.

More rumbling occurred, but it was not the sound of the ground shaking. It sounded more like a great fire was happening. With fear-filled eyes, Lamia stared at the dragon. It opened its mouth wide, wide enough to swallow a mountain whole. Deep in its throat Lamia could see a light coming forth.

From its giant maw came a roaring blaze. It burned the entire landscape in its path, and scorched the sides of the mountains. It blew away the smoke as if it had never been there. The fire blazed forward, and pieces of the mountains it hit flew off in all directions, an imitation of the pyroclastic flow of volcanoes.

When the inferno reached Procerus Mountain, it hit it directly, and the fire blew out to the sides of the mountain. The city was unharmed, though the edges were singed slightly by the flames. The force of the fire pushed the airship Lamia was on forward a great distance, far and fast enough to where they were nearly over Orbis Sea, which was a great distance away.

The other airship had not been so lucky. They had been traveling lower and farther back than Lamia's airship, and it was caught in the all-consuming inferno. The burning of the gnomes onboard was a sight Lamia thankfully missed, due to them lagging behind.

The flames stopped, as did the airship. They were now directly over Orbis Sea, but were still able to see the dragon's head, as well as a small portion of Iugosus. Lamia feared for her comrades, especially Silen. At least she was out of harm's way, which she knew was what Silen cared about most.

What is happening? Astrum thought. After being caught in a great cloud of smoke, a fire had blown it all away, along with Astrum. The force of it, even though most of it was stopped by the mountain, pushed him back several meters, but he was able to catch himself from flying too far.

He had seen the appearance of the grand dragon's horns, but Procerus Mountain blocked most of the creature's head. Hurriedly, he sprinted to Neque, who had been walking in the direction of the beast ever since it had appeared.

Neque did not say a word as Astrum came beside him. He kept a stoic pace towards the great dragon, his mind seemingly far away. Astrum followed close behind, wondering what Neque was going to do.

Chapter 21

The True Monstrosity

Why...have...I...awoken...?
My...slumber...was...not...to...be...broken.
Who...has...placed...the...curse...of...awareness...upon...me...once...again? *My thoughts are...coalescing. I sense...power...drawing near.*

The thoughts of the grand dragon were distant from one another. It tried slowly to regain its control over them. He did not know what had stirred him from his sleep. The weak fire he had breathed out before had helped to clear his throat, although he had forgotten how to speak.

He stayed still for quite some time, trying to

The True Monstrosity

remember how to control his body. He was able to move each of his limbs, as well as his wings and tail, though it seemed that they were held down by some unknown force. He looked towards them, and saw that his entire body, save for his head, was submerged in water.

The power he had felt before came closer, until it seemed that it was directly under him. He turned his attention to it. Below him, he saw two insignificant beings, many times smaller than himself. He opened his mouth a fraction, and breathed out an icy blast of air. It froze the nearby vicinity, as well as the two creatures.

Satisfied, he started to turn back towards his body, but still felt the power of the beings below him. Perplexed, he looked at them once more.

They had both broken free of the ice, and advanced towards him once again. This time, he breathed out a small amount of poisonous gas. They kept advancing. He tried acid, but they bathed in it as if it was water.

The dragon shifted through his entire range of breath weapons. Lava, sand, air, water, lightning, steam, hail, bile, sludge, venom. He pressurized the air, changed the force of gravity, tried to paralyze them, blasted magick upon them, bathed them in darkness, sprayed them with petrifying gas, eroded their skin, pierced them with light, enveloped them in a metallic gas. He changed the weather, called down small meteors, shifted the earth around them, bombarded them with sound, and a vast amount of other different breaths. Though some of the attacks had forced the beings back, they did not appear to be harmed in anyway, though the small plain they were in, as well as some of the closer peaks, was ruined and razed beyond recognition.

Finally, he turned to his greatest breath weapon of all; the breath of time. He blasted them with a small amount, just enough to age them each thousands of years. The upturned ground around them turned into sand, the air itself decayed with age, and the mountains surrounding them crumbled down, some erupting as they turned into volcanoes. The two beings pressed on, ignoring this as if it were the breath of a small wind.

The dragon's confusion turned to pure wonder as the beings kept their steady pace. They had unsheathed their swords, as if they were going to slay him. He snorted; a booming sound not dissimilar to thunder.

"Puny beings," the great dragon whispered, though his voice was still deafening. "What is it you come for? Why do you not disappear? I am the holder of every breath weapon, the guardian of this land, and the destroyer of it. I have prevented anything from approaching this island, as well as preventing some to leave. The tides themselves bend to my will, even in slumber. My duty was to protect this land, until such a time when it needed to be decimated. Do you think you have enough power to stop me? I am the Keeper of Worlds, the Maw of Death, the Ultimate Dragon. I have lived for thousands of years, and will live for thousands more."

"I AM REX REGIS," the dragon roared, his voice reaching volumes of great intensity.

Rex Regis lifted a single claw from the ocean. The emergence of his finger created large waves; each large enough to reach the top of the cliff the two beings were on. He raised his claw high, and brought it down upon

The True Monstrosity

them. They raised their swords in tandem, creating a cross to block his claw. He laughed inwardly at their audacity.

He struck them, but was stopped. Their swords had stopped his claw, though he was stronger by far. Or so he thought. In retaliation, they both struck at his finger, and they cut deep into his flesh.

Rex Regis reared back in surprise, unaware that there was something that could pierce his skin. Both of the beings' swords stuck in his finger as he pulled it away, and they traveled upwards with it. He flicked his finger, and they flew high above him. One, however, grew wings, and stopped his ascent, while the other kept flying upwards.

The being with the wings dove towards the dragon, and came down to his eye. The being struck at it with his blue sword, but Rex Regis was able to blink just in time to prevent his eye from being hit. The sword cut the eyelid, and the dragon growled in pain and fury.

The other being finally descended, and landed on the dragon's snout. He plunged his sword into Rex Regis' skin, and ran with it, cleaving his flesh from his nose to the top of his head. Rex Regis did not know what to do to these indestructible beings to stop their rampage.

Then, as if hesitating, the two beings stopped their attack on the dragon. They stood upon his vast head, staying quite still. Suddenly, they ran towards each other, and locked their swords together. They had ceased their attack on Rex Regis to fight amongst themselves.

What odd circumstance is this? Rex Regis thought. He knew now the two beings held power to destroy him, yet stopped doing so to fight one another. He stood still, letting them fight. He was not arrogant as the others of his race; he knew he could not win against them from the small display of power they had shown. Perhaps they would demolish each other, saving Rex Regis from death. The only thing the grand dragon feared was forces unknown to him, and these two beings qualified.

They fought for several hours, neither of them letting up the assault on the other. Rex Regis did not know the specifics of the fight, although it felt as though they were equal in power and speed. On several occasions he tilted his head slightly, to give one advantage over the other, though it did not seem to matter, for still they clashed.

The dragon could not give up on killing them, however. As soon as their fight was done, he would strike at the remaining combatant.

Astrum had been awed when he had seen the dragon, though he realized quickly that he must destroy it. Neque, it seemed, held the same idea in mind. The destructive forces of the dragon were great, but luckily it was focused on the two immortals, so a large portion of the mountain range, including Procerus, was not harmed. The most amount of damage that happened to the mountains was when the dragon had first breathed fire upon them. The west side of most of the mountains had turned black after being burned as they had.

Astrum and Neque had then fought the dragon for

some time, but soon turned on each other when it seemed that the beast could do nothing against them.

Upon Rex Regis' head they battled. It was a very wide space, due to the dragon's immense size. The diamond-like skin of the dragon was very smooth, and after many millennia of being underwater each individual scale had been dulled, yet they retained their hardness, which was akin to a diamond.

The fight against Neque was not arriving at a conclusion soon. Several times the dragon shifted its head slightly, but it did not aid the fight in either of their favors. The battle could theoretically rage on forever.

After a particularly powerful set of blows against one another's swords, they stood together, swords locked against one another. Again, Astrum felt a slight pull as their swords touched, and they each glowed bright with their respective colors.

"Why do you persist, Neque?" Astrum asked, wanting the battle to end so he could attend to the dragon.

"Persist? You are the one who started this." Neque retorted. "The dragons could have destroyed Iugosus and that would have been that. You are the one who confronted me, wanting to fight. I did not want this."

Astrum snorted in laughter. "You want to have nature reclaim Solum, and have dragons rule. The races, for one, would not stand for that, as it would mean many deaths, and I do not stand for it, either." Astrum felt the attraction between the blades grow stronger as more time passed, though Neque seemed to not realize it.

"The dragons were here first, and they lived peacefully. Once the races came, war started almost immediately." Neque said regretfully. "It would have been in the dragon's favor had you not isolated me as you did."

Astrum cocked his head, and adopted a confused face. "I remember doing no such thing." Astrum replied, truthfully. After a certain point in the past, he remembered nothing.

Neque sighed, a very dismal sound. "Of course you do not. Why would you?"

With that said, Neque tried to pull away his sword, but found he could not. He tried again, tugging on it with more force, but he could not wrench it free of Astrum's sword, despite his immense power.

Suddenly, Neque's sword seemed to be consumed by and merge with Astrum's blade. The swords melded together, the metal shifting and changing like liquid. Neque backed away as he saw Medius being consumed by Aevum.

Astrum stared at his blade. It had stopped transforming, and grew still. The blade was longer by several inches, and was slightly wider. The hilt grew as well, and changed from a pure white to a light blue, and the gem present in the pommel was now half green and half light blue. The cross guard grew downwards slightly, instead of being straight, as it had been.

Astrum stopped admiring the blade and turned his attention on Neque, who seemed to have a small tear in his eye. Astrum stabbed forward with his sword, piercing Neque's heart. Neque gasped slightly, surprised by the pain. He then sank to his knees, his

The True Monstrosity

head slumping downwards.

Neque began to fade away. Small pinpricks of a cyan glow came from his body, and rose into the air. The light changed its course, and flew into Astrum's body. As the light transferred itself from Neque to Astrum, visions flew through Astrum's mind, though they seemed more like memories.

There was Neque, standing on top of a large piece of land. They seemed to be high, but it did not have the appearance of the top of a mountain. They faced each other, and Neque was weeping softly. Dragons flew around them, roaring. Astrum walked to Neque, and placed its hand on Neque's shoulder, as if in comfort.

Neque looked behind Astrum, and he followed his gaze. Behind them was a woman wearing a long white dress, with long blonde hair. She turned to Neque and Astrum, and her face was emotionless. She grew wings, and flew off.

Astrum faced Neque once more. Neque watched the woman leave, and sank down to his knees. Astrum placed his hand on Neque's head for a moment, but then walked away. He walked past several large ruins, as well as a house, where inside he could hear the small sounds of a baby dragon. Astrum walked to the edge of the land, and peered down below. For many miles around all he could see was water.

Then he dove off, and plummeted below, into the sea.

Astrum sighed. Neque's body had vanished completely. From Astrum's back he felt something peculiar. He turned his head to look, and found that he now possessed dragonfly-like wings, much the same as Neque had owned. He fluttered them, and then made them disappear from view. He flexed his hand, and felt new power flow into him. It seemed he had regained some magickal power, and had become stronger. Did he absorb Neque in some way?

Astrum hefted his sword, and rested it on his shoulder. He walked to the dragon's snout, and walked off the edge.

Rex Regis did not feel the presence of one of the beings, though the other had become much stronger with its passing. He felt the remaining being walk to the edge of his nose, and then jumped off.

A small distance from the dragon's head he saw the being. It was the flightless one, but he seemed to now possess the wings of the other. Rex Regis stared at him intently.

"What now, being? What is it you seek to do?" Rex Regis questioned, truly wishing to know.

The being sighed, and pointed his sword towards Rex Regis. "I seek your ruination."

Rex Regis laughed heartily, the rumblings in his throat filling the entire mountain range. "I may not be able to harm you, but you will not kill me. To do such a thing, you have to possess powers of a god!" the dragon thundered, not even considering the prospect to be true.

The being chuckled in response. "My name is Astrum, wielder of the sword of Aevum, of life and death. You want to know something?"

The dragon tilted his head slightly in bemusement. "That comment you made was something that I did not

The True Monstrosity

believe possible myself, but a soothsayer told me otherwise, not too long ago."

Rex Regis' eyes grew wide as he realized the enormity of what Astrum had stated. Astrum laughed again, but not a joyous one; instead it was filled with sorrow. His face grew serious, and his blade glowed with a light blue and green light.

Rex Regis reared backwards to try and flee the man, but to no avail. Astrum concentrated what magick he had into his blade, and swung upward with all his might.

From the blade a large crescent of magick was let loose. It hit the dragon's head, biting deep into the side. The flesh separated slightly, revealing the inside of the dragon's head. Blood flowed uncontrollably from the fatal blow, spraying the landscape and the ocean a deep red.

Astrum floated in the air above the falling dragon's head, which created a humongous wave as it hit the ocean surface. Rex Regis' lifeless head floated for a moment, and then sunk back into the depths, large torrents of water flowing into the gaping wound.

Chapter 22

Prelude to a New Beginning

Astrum soared over the landscape. The newfound freedom the wings granted him was exhilarating. He was able to climb to the highest of heights, over the mountains, and then dive like a falcon towards the ground. The wings were more powerful than they seemed. The clouds had evaporated beforehand due to the intense heat of Rex Regi's flame, leaving the air completely clear.

After several more minutes of flying through the air, he stopped midair and admired the view.

The land all around him was desolate. The small plain near the ocean had turned to red sand, while the mountains closest by where Rex Regis had appeared had crumbled to a fraction of their original height. The breath weapon of time was surely terrifying; against all that is mortal or inanimate, that is. Astrum chuckled.

Astrum looked across Orbis Sea. He saw the Pluvia mountain range that bordered the opposite side of the ocean, blocking most of the Infelix desert from sight. He saw the human plains, as well as Montis Mountain in the distance. The volcanoes to the left of him signified the realm of the dimidium, and the forests to the right the elven realm.

Peering around closer to him, he spotted Mount Procerus, and started to make his way towards it. The side of every mountain Astrum could see had been completely scorched by the dragon's initial fire. The mountains were all blackened, and as Astrum passed by them, he could see that the other side of each seemed completely fine. It was as if the mountain was made out of two different types of rocks.

Astrum reached Procerus, and flew over it and the city. As he looked down, he saw that the troops guarding the castle had all disappeared, presumably to take shelter from the dragon inside the mountain. He knew not the losses that had occurred, but he sense that none of his companions had been harmed, and that was enough.

He searched the sky for the airship, and spotted one coming back from the east. He flew to it, which took several minutes, and landed on the deck, eliciting a small cry of shock from Lamia. She ran over to him and embraced him, laughing, with tears of joy rolling down her face. Gelu walked over and patted Astrum on the back, in between his new wings. Astrum made them disappear into his back, much like he had seen Neque and Lumen do.

"What happened?" Lamia asked, wiping the tears from her face.

"I will tell you as soon as everyone is gathered together. Where is everyone else?" Astrum asked.

Lamia proceeded to tell him all the events that had happened that she knew of. She told him of Vis also gaining power of flight, and how he and Silen had traveled to the castle to "meet" with the dwarven king. She recalled that Nauto and Lex had both invaded the city along with the army, but had not heard from them yet. Lamia recounted the fear the dragons had held when the monstrosity arose from the ocean, and how they had fled. Then she told him how the great dragon's fire had launched the airship out to Orbis Sea, while the other had perished in the blaze.

Astrum listened to her recount what had happened; he glad to hear that no one seemed to have been harmed. Indoles walked up to them after Lamia had finished.

"We must go to the kingdom at once!" Indoles excitedly chimed. Astrum chuckled, nodding his head in agreement.

While Lamia, Gelu, and Indoles discussed what their next move was to be, Astrum walked to the prow of the airship, admiring the view. When facing the mountains, none of the damage the fire had done could be seen, save for the sides appearing to be blackened. Far out, near the ocean, he could see some of the desolation Rex Regis had committed against Astrum and Neque, but everything else seemed to be largely in order.

He peered below him, and saw something that sunk his joy.

Marching across the plains below Procerus mountains was a countless number of dwarves. The force came from mountains that surrounded the plains in front of Procerus. *Why had they not been in the city?* Astrum wondered. Each of the dwarves appeared to be wearing armor, and all held some manner of weaponry, although the army seemed to be a bit odd, for some reason. Astrum did not know why, but he realized that after the events that had befallen the area, the elven/human army would be in disarray.

Astrum laughed as he realized the situation. Without a saying a word to Lamia, Gelu, or the gnomish king, he dove off of the airship.

Above him he heard the gasp from Lamia, but then the rushing of the wind canceled out all other noises. The air was now his domain, as much so as the land. He unfurled his unorthodox wings, and swooped towards the front of the army. Below him, the dwarves fell to the ground, gasped, or shrieked as he flew over them.

Astrum reached the front lines, traveled upwards slightly, and then made his wings vanish into his back. He dropped down to the ground, making it crack slightly under the force of his landing.

After a moment of crouching, he stood up tall, and unsheathed his sword slowly. The terror-filled eyes of the dwarves almost seemed comical. His blade crackled with arcane energy. He cracked a crooked smile, and rested his blade upon his shoulder.

Several tense moments passed, and everyone was

still. Astrum shifted slightly in discomfort, his smile slowly fading. With a great roar surpassed only by that of Rex Regis, the dwarves surged forward, ready to battle him.

Much better, Astrum thought.

He adopted a feral grin, crouched down slightly, not unlike a tiger. With a great bound, he jumped into the fray, his laugh sounding like the snarl of a fierce beast.

He sat in his throne of ebony and ivory, contemplating the unfolding events quietly. His hands were in the shape of a temple, and He rested His elbows upon His knees. The dragon had been defeated easily, with little loss to Astrum. In fact, Astrum had only gained from the encounter. Astrum had been reunited with a part of himself. Astrum was advancing quickly, far faster than He had thought he would.

He sighed, sat back upon his throne. His eyes glinted a bright violet. He placed his head into his hand, as if tired.

"Come unto me, O Fallen Star. Meet your fate here, in the Aether of the world. I will wait while you regain yourself down below. When you are prepared, I will send for thee. The emissary of the heavens will come to you, and you will accept its summons, willingly or no. Battle your way through the halls of eternity, and confront me in my domain. I will wait for you, Astrum, for your homecoming will spell the end of the world. Prodigal being, return so that I, Deus, may reign over the universe."

Prelude to a New Beginning

"My light shall outshine yours, as you are a mere reflection of me, after all." He added, almost gleefully.

He laughed, and the large white room he was in shook with the intensity of his diabolical glee. The fervor of His laugh shook the walls of the very existence of the room, making them shudder in such a way that it seemed that they might cave in at any time.

Deus ceased his laughter, and all was still.